Daniel C. Eddy

The young man's friend, containing adminitions for the erring, counsel for the tempted, hope for the fallen

Daniel C. Eddy

The young man's friend, containing adminitions for the erring, counsel for the tempted, hope for the fallen

ISBN/EAN: 9783337102135

Printed in Europe, USA, Canada, Australia, Japan

Cover: Foto ©Andreas Hilbeck / pixelio.de

More available books at **www.hansebooks.com**

THE

YOUNG MAN'S FRIEND;

CONTAINING

ADMONITIONS FOR THE ERRING, COUNSEL FOR THE
TEMPTED, HOPE FOR·THE FALLEN.

DESIGNED FOR

The Young Man,

The Husband,

And the Father.

By DANIEL C. EDDY, D.D.,
PASTOR OF THE BALDWIN PLACE CHURCH, BOSTON.

I have written unto you, young men, because ye are strong. JOHN.

NEW EDITION.

BOSTON:
HORACE WENTWORTH,
119 WASHINGTON STREET.
18

PREFACE.

$\mathfrak{T}$HIS volume is given to the public, by the advice of some of the author's most judicious friends, who cherish the hope that it may be the means of shielding.the young from crime and leading them to the practice of virtue and the pursuit of holiness.

The lectures were originally delivered to a large congregation of young men, and it has been thought best, that the direct, personal appeal of the pulpit should be retained, and such alterations only, made, as would adapt them to general circulation.

The object of the book is, to impress upon the minds of young men, such lessons of virtue as will render them useful and successful in life, and by presenting the old Puritan view of sinful pleasures, lead the reader to cultivate the old Puritan integrity.

While innocent amusements have been encouraged, dangerous amusements have been condemned, and the mind directed to healthy, reasonable sources of recreation, which have been furnished so amply by nature and by God — amusements which embrace utility with recreation, and pleasure with profit.

An effort has been made to blend instruction with exhortation — encouragement with warning, and by holding up, side by side, the woes of vice and the rewards of virtue, lead the young to hate the one, and love the other.

The earnest wish, and fervent prayer of the author is, that the work may *do good*, and prove a source of profit to the young men into whose hands it may chance to fall.

CONTENTS.

LECTURE I.

THE ELEMENTS OF A MANLY COURSE.

PAGE

Wealth, birth, intellect, do not constitute manliness. An effort for the promotion of virtue. An interest in the elevation of the race. Submission to the demands of God. . 13

LECTURE II.

YOUTH; ITS ADVANTAGES AND DISADVANTAGES.

Formation of character. Napoleon. Doddridge. Baxter. The mistakes of youth. The ardor of youth. Youth is a period of great results. Alexander. Cortes. Bacon. Newton. Pitt. Calvin. Melancthon. Pope. Dwight. Adams. 35

LECTURE III.

FOUR SOURCES OF SUCCESS IN LIFE.

Industry. Dignity of labor. Uses of labor. Frugality. Small expenses. Temperance. Illustrations. Honesty. Worth of character. The rewards of honesty. 57

LECTURE IV.

INNOCENT AMUSEMENTS.

Need of recreation. Causes of the failure to secure amusement. Utility must be combined with pleasure. Useful reading. Music. Travelling. Literary Lectures. Social visiting. Social gatherings. Paintings, and other works of art. Public and private worship. 80

LECTURE V.

DANGEROUS AMUSEMENTS.

The theatre. Dancing. Gambling. Social drinking. Objections to them. They abuse time. Destroy health. Lead to prodigality. They are heart-corrupting. They are soul-destroying. 104

LECTURE VI.

WEALTH AND FAME.

They are fluctuating and uncertain. Louis XVI. Marie Antoinette. Napoleon. Louis Philippe. Pius IX. They fail to secure happiness. Rich and poor men. They lead to crime if unreasonably loved. They are as brief as life. Saladin. Philip. 128

LECTURE VII.

GAMBLING.

A system of prodigality. It excites, intoxicates, and maddens the brain. It is the highway to idleness. It is a system of falsehood — of theft. It nullifies the marriage relation. Produces confusion in families. Instances of its effects. Leads to intemperance. Destroys kind and tender feelings. Corrupts society. Illustrations. 152

LECTURE VIII.

INTEMPERANCE.

Produces poverty. Ruins the constitution. Destroys domestic felicity. Produces idiocy and madness. Excludes from heaven. Cases to illustrate. A plea to young men. . . 175

LECTURE IX.

THE DETECTION OF SIN CERTAIN.

The probability and certainty of it. The confessions of associates. The power of memory. The upbraidings of conscience. The providence of God. The bed of death. Every sin seen by God. The coming judgment. Illustrations of these truths. Concluding appeal. 200

LECTURE X.

THE BIBLE A PERFECT GUIDE.

In all life's duties. Duties to ourselves — to kindred and friends — to fellow-men — to government — to God. A guide in cases of danger — from error — from crime — from sin — from misery. Good and great men have loved the Bible. It has claims as a book of history and poetry. It is a divine revelation. 219

PUBLISHERS' NOTICE.

In editions prior to 1866, we published, of the four following books, more than one hundred and forty thousand of the " YOUNG MAN'S FRIEND; " of the " YOUNG WOMAN'S FRIEND," published four years later, over fifty thousand; more than one hundred thousand of the " ANGEL WHISPERS," and seventy-five thousand of the " HEROINES OF THE CHURCH," under another title. We now propose arranging these works in sets, uniform in size and style of binding. The " HEROINES OF THE CHURCH " has been republished in England and Holland, and many thousands sold. Rev. Dr. Cumming, of London, in editing the English edition of this work, says : " This little volume appears to me likely to enlarge and augment the labors of Christian females, to evince to the Church of Christ their value, and the duty of availing herself of their precious resources yet more extensively, and to make us more deeply grateful to God that his grace has raised up for us Christian females, notwithstanding our insensibility to their worth, who have proved themselves examples of tenderness, zeal, and successful missionary exertions."

THE YOUNG MAN'S FRIEND.

LECTURE I.

THE ELEMENTS OF A MANLY COURSE.

Show thyself a man. 1 *Kings*, ii. 2.

THIS was a part of the royal David's dying charge to Solomon his son. The monarch minstrel was about to be gathered to his fathers, the door of the sepulchre was open for him, and his grave clothes were ready. The crown he had already placed upon the head of his youngest son, and as he stood with one foot in the grave, and one upon the crumbling shores of time, he enjoined with all a father's solicitude, the performance of those duties and the observance of those rules, which were well calculated to render his government perpetual, and his name illustrious. He exhorted him, not to show himself a warrior merely — not a statesman merely — not a monarch merely, but a MAN — possessing the generous impulses of a man, and displaying a manly nature in all his intercourse with men. So Solomon understood him, and his government became the admiration of the world, his fame spread through all nations, and the proudest monarchs of the earth came to behold his glory, and the magnificence of his kingdom. While others reigned as kings, and ruled as tyrants, he governed as a man, having common sympathies with those above whom he had been elevated by birth and blood.

In our times, there are various and contradictory opinions cherished, in regard to what constitutes *a manly course.* It is not every one that wears a human form that can claim to be a man, in the full sense of that term, though he may prove his connection with the human race. Many live and move among us who are destitute of the chief elements of a manly character. They suppose themselves men indeed — they regard their own course as honorable and worthy of imitation. The gambler has his code of honor; the duellist has his code of honor; the soldier red in blood has his code of honor. Napoleon was an honorable man in his way, and the world ascribed to him many great and noble qualities. He fought well, and conquered well. His banner waved in triumph over many a bloody field ; carnage, and famine, and death attended his steps, and like the genius of evil he stalked abroad. He was, doubtless, a splendid general and a brilliant emperor; but the child who wandered over the field after his most triumphant charge, and wet with water the lips of the dying soldier there, was far more exalted in the scale of being, than was the plumed and epauletted chieftain.

Nelson was a skilful officer, and died as the world says, " in all his glory." His banner was his shroud; the roar of cannon was his dirge, and the shout of victory was his requiem. In the history of naval heroes, his name stands foremost, and they who love the navy, have learned to honor him. But the poor sailor, who a few months since in yonder distant city, braved the fire, and at the risk of his own life saved a mother's only child, gained a truer glory than ever shone around the victories of the distinguished admiral.

How false — how unjust the estimate which the world places upon the actions of men. He who dies upon the battle field — who rushes to carnage and to strife — whose hands are dripping with human gore, is a man of honor. Parliaments and senates return him thanks, and whole nations unite in erecting a monument over the spot where sleeps his corpse. But he whose task it is, to dry up the stream of blood, — to mitigate the anguish of earth, — to lift man up, and make him what God designed him to be, dies without a tongue to speak his eulogy, or a monument to mark his fall. That only is truly honorable which does good to the body or the soul of man — which contributes to human happiness, or promotes the glory of God. He shows himself a man, and he only, who sacrifices his own interests that he may benefit others — who lives unknown to fame that he may bind up some broken heart — who lays his own honor and happiness, and even life itself, upon the altar of a common humanity.

My reader, would you show yourself a man, go not to yonder tented field, where death hovers, and the vulture feasts himself upon human victims! Go not where men are carving monuments of marble to perpetuate names which will not live in one grateful memory! Go not to the dwellings of the rich! Go not to the palaces of kings! Go not to the halls of merriment and pleasure! Go to the widow and relieve her woe: Go to the orphan and speak words of comfort: Go to the lost and save him: Go to the fallen and raise him up: Go to the wanderer and bring him back to virtue: Go to the sinner and whisper in his ears words of salvation and eternal life.

The true object of life has scarcely begun to be understood. In past ages men have been attracted by the glitter and show of conquest, and worldly predominance. They have pursued the phantom, while the real and the substantial have been sacrificed.

They have aimed at the accomplishment of objects, which have resulted in no good to the world. They have built up systems of monstrous wrong. They have strengthened the dominion of human cruelty and labored more to crush the race than to lift it up. SELF has been the common centre, and around it the universe has been made to revolve like systems around their suns. What, then, are the elements of true manliness?

Wealth is not one. In a multitude of cases the possessor of the largest fortune, and the widest territory, has been found to have views and feelings not at all in proportion to the magnitude of his fortune. There is a contingency about wealth which has nothing to do with moral or intellectual character. It seems to be rained upon the human family by a capricious goddess, who distributes her favors according to rules known only to herself. At one time a monarch is her favorite, and his throne she studs with jewels, and fills his crown with richest diamonds. At his feet she spreads out broad fields — well cultivated vineyards — beautiful temples and shining towers, and as his admiring eye gazes over the scene, she whispers in his ear, — " These are thine! " At another time she fixes her eye upon a beggar boy, as he asks for food from house to house, repulsed everywhere. His hand she takes, and leads him up, as if by magic through the various grades of society until she establishes him

2

in a palace, and fills his coffers with the shining gold.
Fair cheeked young men have sought to win her
smile, but sought in vain, while she has turned from
them to bestow her gifts upon some unsightly being,
on whom God's curse seems to have fallen.   The intelligent — the virtuous — the brave — the wise,
have knelt at her altar, and breathed their supplications, but she has spurned them away and beckoned
with friendly hand, to sordid ignorance and vice.
Hence we find that wealth gives us no clue to character — furnishes us with no criterion by which we may
measure the soul, and judge of the dimensions of the
man himself.

Birth and blood are not elements of true manliness.
Royal veins are often found to flow with plebeian
streams, and crime and duplicity as often disgrace the
palace of the monarch, as the hovel of the slave.
Cæsar was a monarch.   Blood of which after ages
loved to boast, flowed through his princely temples.
A crown was on his brow — the imperial crown.   At
the foot of his throne proud nations nestled, and o'er
all the earth his banner waved; but was Cæsar a
man? had he a manly character? was his bosom
thrilled by manly emotions?   No.   Nero's heart
swelled with the blood of emperors.   Rome acknowledged him as her sovereign; but was he a man? No.
Nero and Cæsar were both monarchs, but they were
not men in the noblest sense.   No living link con-

nccted them with the great heart of humanity. They were on earth — they ate and drank and slept like other men — they wore the human form, but aside from this, they moved like demons through the earth, smiting its flowers and withering its verdure. When they descended from the living to the dead, a mighty incubus was removed from the crushed form of humanity, and upon their graves she stood and uttered thanksgiving. On the other hand, we have seen beggars and slaves in whose veins not a single drop of princely blood was flowing, come forth from their low abodes to startle the world with the brilliancy of their lives, wake up the race to angelic deeds and produce a wonderful change throughout all the ranks of men, and all grades of human society. Such was Luther. He was no prince. He bore no tokens of royalty. He came clad in no habiliments of state and majesty. From a cloistered cell he came — a shaven monk. In his hand no sceptre — on his head no crown. But he had a human heart within him, and it gushed out for human woe. Such was Wilberforce and Howard and Carey and a host of others, who have stood for right, and breasted the world's dark tide for the good of men.

Intellect does not make the man. I admit the power of intellect. I acknowledge its superiority over wealth, physical power, and brute force; but a mere intellectualist is not a man. True, intellect is one of the elements which enter into the composition of man, as we usually apply that term; but in the better sense in which I use the word, *the possession* of intellect only, gives proof that one is fitted to be a man, and *the use* of that intellect shows to what extent he *is* a man.   Enter any department of literature and science, and you will find men of vast power and might.   Among the poets, you behold Byron standing in the first rank.   The grasp of thought — the clear conception — the elevated diction — the elegant language, are seen at a single glance.   As an intellectualist, he stands almost beyond the power of criticism, and that is a bold man who dares hurl a shaft at the literary merits of his productions.   But what is the tendency of the works of Byron ?   Will his writings do good or evil ?   I hesitate not to say, as other men have said before me, that they tend to corruption, — that they are calculated to sink the feelings of the reader,—lower the standard of his virtues, — corrupt his taste and deprave his heart.   Among historians, stands conspicuously the name of Gibbon.   And what was he ?   From every quarter of the globe, I hear the reply, " He was one of the world's most distinguished writers."   His " Decline and Fall of the Roman Empire," will continue to be read with interest so long as the world stands — his name will be remembered as long as time endures.   But Gibbon was a sceptic as well as a historian.   His works are full of artful attacks up·

on the religion of the cross. Scepticism is interwoven with all that he has written, and to the last age will be handed down with his grand history, his attempts to undermine the Bible, and overthrow the Christian faith. While literature will point to him as one of its most distinguished ornaments, Christianity will pronounce the name of Edward Gibbon with tears of pity. Poetry and history are not the only departments which furnish such instances. On every page of the book of fame, are found the names of men endowed by God with giant minds — men of dazzling intellect, who have used their powers for the perversion of truth and the destruction of the kingdom of Christ. Look at Bulwer and Alexander Dumas! what powers of mind! what vast capacity for labor! what unwearied perseverance in catering to the public taste; and all perverted — all used to debase man, and sink him to a level with the brutes. Towering intellect, when used for unholy purposes — when made a minister of vice, is a curse, not only to its possessor but to all who come within the circle of its fatal influence: and better would it be for the world to be without these splendid intellects than to have them devoted to the service of Satan.

In enforcing the exhortation of David to his son, upon your minds my readers, I wish to present three ways in which each one may show himself a man in the highest meaning of that term, and which if observed will promote happiness in this life and lead to glory in the life to come. As I make these remarks, I remember that I am a young man myself—that a mutual sympathy must exist between myself and the younger portion of my congregation—that we are sailing over life together, and hence have common interests, common hopes, and common dangers. I will urge you then to show yourself a man,

I. BY A MANLY EFFORT FOR THE PROMOTION OF VIRTUE. Society cannot exist without virtue. It is impossible for a vicious and depraved community to be prosperous and happy. God has otherwise ordained. He has made virtue the basis of happiness, and vice the cause of sorrow. With communities, as well as with individuals, the sentiment of Scripture proves true, "The way of the transgressor is hard." Hence, if we look back over the history of the past, we find nations and communities prosperous and happy, just in proportion to the public and private virtues of the people. We find the ancient republics while devoted to virtue, rising in opulence and increasing in honor and happiness. We behold them increasing their influence; spreading their conquests, and ex tending their authority. But in process of time those . republics became corrupt; the virtue of the people died out, the temples were consecrated to crime, and the altars stained with blood. As vice increased, the bright dream of happiness vanished before its dark

and dreadful form, and one by one those nations,
once the admiration of the world, have fallen into ruin.
Where are they now? Their blackened pillars —
their crumbling temples — their ruined honor, their
fallen greatness, alone remain as warning beacons to
all coming time. The principle remains unchanged.
Virtue is now the basis of happiness and prosperity,
and the nation which discards it, will speedily sink into ruin. France has been tampering with it for years,
and the result has been fearful. Revolution after
revolution has occurred — one wave of blood after
another has rolled through the guilty streets of Paris,
and the people from one end of the land to the other,
have been clothed in mourning. In our own land, —
in all our cities, — a warfare between virtue and vice
is in continual progress. The discordant elements of
one, and the pure principles of the other, are at work,
striving for universal conquest. The gigantic form
of evil is stalking abroad, and sin of all grades is
fearfully prevalent. Look around, and you will behold intemperance fondly cherished. You will see
the drunkard reeling and staggering to his fall. You
will see standing at the bar, all characters and conditions in life, from the young man who seems
abashed amid the gay throng, and takes his first
glass with trembling and fear, to the aged drunkard
from whom all shame and contrition have fled away.
Go forth and you will see them reeling out to the

light of day, the son, the brother, the father, and sometimes the wife and mother. Follow them to their abodes, and you will behold their homes divested of all that is attractive, and converted into places of misery. Intemperance is not alone. By its side, marching to this conquest over man, is immorality of every sort, and depravity of every description. The picture which Pollock drew of our world as it will be at the consummation, is too fearfully true at the present time :

> "Satan raged loose, Sin had her will, and Death
> Enough. Blood trod upon the heels of Blood;
> Revenge in desperate mood, at midnight met
> Revenge. War brayed to War, Deceit deceived
> Deceit. Lie cheated Lie, and Treachery,
> Mined under Treachery; and Perjury
> Swore back on Perjury; and Blasphemy
> Arose with hideous Blasphemy, and curse
> Loud answering curse; and drunkard stumbling fell
> O'er drunkard fallen; and husband, husband met
> Returning from each other's bed defiled:
> Thief stole from thief; and robber on the way
> Knocked robber down; and Lewdness, Violence
> And Hate met Lewdness, Violence, and Hate."

The mission of the young man in this age, is, to meet these evils which have crept in upon society, and with all his influence arrest if possible the tide of sin which is sweeping over the world. Vice has its known, open, avowed supporters. Those who are en-gaged in vicious employments — whose craft consists in making men miserable, and preparing their souls for perdition, are using all their endeavors to spread corruption. In some cases the public press and the pulpit, have so far forgotten the dignity connected with them, as to become defenders of crime, and have given their sanction to the progress of the fearful scourge.

Now I cherish the opinion, and in it I think you will concur, that the young men of our country have never taken that position in relation to vice, which it is their sacred duty to occupy. Thus far they have stood aloof, as a body, from the great contest, and have left their grey-haired sires to fight alone. They have felt that it did not belong to them to enter the foremost rank, and stand out in defence of the great principles of right. In this I contend that young men have mistaken their true position. There is no class, to whom a louder call is given by God and humanity, to enter the field as the avowed defenders of virtue and truth. There is no class of persons capable of accomplishing more, and effecting the object with more ease and readiness than are they. Should the young men of our cities in one firm united band set their faces against vice of every description, the effect would be instant and irresistible. Half the dram-shops would be closed, half the gambling-saloons would be deserted, crape would hang upon the door of the theatre, and the grinding of the music in the hall of revelry would become low. And

I ask if such a prospect has nothing attractive to this crowd of young men? Is not the sight of reformed — regenerated drunkards — redeemed gamblers, lib-ertines, and Sabbath-breakers, one worthy of our care and efforts? Is there no music in the song of the mother over her reformed son? Is there no charm in the willing step of the prodigal, as he returns to the home of his youth, and to the bosom of his sire? Is there no beauty to the form of Virtue as she stands with her foot upon the neck of prostrate Vice?

The question will arise in some minds, What can I do? Were I in the ministry, or did I stand at the head of one of the learned professions, the attempt might be successful. Let such a young man look at the instances in which young men, and old men, have ac-complished great results under the most discouraging circumstances. Let him turn his eye to Luther as from his cell he came, and hurled his shafts at Rome. Let him behold Columbus as he chartered his ves-sel, and hired his crew, and sailed forth, jeered and scorned, to discover a new world. Let him contem-plate the numberless cases of like character which adorn the history of the world, and learn from them, that a young man can do anything that is right.

II. BY A MANLY INTEREST IN THE ELEVATION OF THE RACE. We sustain certain relations to the whole human family. We are children of one common pa-rent. We are the heirs of one common inheritance.

Go to the wildest spot on earth, and find the blackest character which exists within the limits of the race, and you find in that dark character, a relative — *a brother.* Ethiopia's son as he lifts his hands to God — the wild Karen as he rushes from his dark jungle, ready for blood — the child of Erin, as he comes in rags and poverty to our shores, are all our brethren. We cannot divest ourselves of this relationship if we would. God has formed it for us, and whether we are willing to acknowledge the fact or not, the race is one wide and indissoluble fraternity. The black faced negro — the hunted Indian and the proudest child of civilization, are of one blood. Hence we find that God has given us a natural sympathy one with another. He has created us with a feeling of relationship, and given us a disposition to assist the fallen, and relieve the wants of the needy. He has designed that we should be mutual helpers and assistants, and has placed us in a position of mutual dependence, so that our relations may ever be recognised.

It is when man is displaying himself for the good of others that he seems most Godlike, and if there is a time when he appears to have but little of the influence of depravity in his heart, it is, when ministering like an angel of mercy to the wants and woes of life. Now in the providence of God it has occurred, that the young men of America are more favorably situated, than are the young men of any other portion of the earth. Thanks to God and the Puritans, we occupy a spot on which intelligence, morality, and religion have shed their mildest beams, and exerted their most happy influences. Consequently we can look abroad and behold everywhere the objects of pity and commiseration. Ignorance, slavery, heathenish degradation, arrest the attention everywhere, and pathetic appeals from every quarter are made to the young men of our own favored section of the earth. Nor have we a right to deny these claims and resist these appeals. The object for which we live, is not to secure our own gratification, and minister to our own increasing desires. The good of others should be one of the most prominent objects of our lives — an object never to be forgotten. He who has never felt his bosom thrill with pity at the recital of scenes which are transpiring upon the earth, he who has not gazed with feelings of deep commiseration upon the millions who sit in darkness and in the shadow of death, and who has never made an effort to send them the means of civilization, and the religion of the cross, is a stranger to the emotions which will crowd upon the mind of every man, who understands his relations to his fellow-creatures, and who is willing to acknowledge them.

Whatever may be our views of Christianity, whatever may be our opinion of experimental piety, we cannot but admit our obligation to send the Bible to all climes.

Thus far the influence of Christianity upon the nations of the earth has been inconceivably great. It has
swept away system after system of philosophy, politics,
and religion. It has remodeled the whole framework
of human society — upturned its very foundations, and
laid at the basis of all earthly intercourse, principles
new and hitherto unknown. Before Christianity, the
Jews had a ritual of blood, and the heathen a ritual
of darkness. Christ sealed up the fountain of one,
and the exploded dogmas of past ages gave place
to the sublime faith of the Son of God. And such
ever will be the influence of the gospel wherever it is
propagated. It will dissipate darkness — dispel the
gloom of mind — break the fetters of the slave, and
make virtuous and happy society.

Such being the nature of Christianity, it is the duty
of young men to send it to the heathen, whether they
have themselves embraced it, or not. Whatever may
be our opinion of its influence upon the soul of man,
all agree that it embraces the only system of morality
which can render the world happy, and the governments of the earth glorious. Consequently it is our
duty, to send to heathen nations the Bible, that
it may civilize and make them moral, and he who
casts his influence against the missionary enterprise,
casts it not only against the salvation of the souls of
the heathen, but against the progress of civilization,
and hence, is an enemy of his race, and forfeits his

claim to the name of man. Our relations to others are not understood as they ought to be. The mass of young men seem to feel that they are under no obligation to aid in the elevation of the race. But is it so? God and humanity give a negative reply. The young have no right to rest from toil, until want is driven from the borders of our own country, until virtue is respected, and vice hated, until labor receives its due reward, until honest men are respected whatever may be their pecuniary circumstances, until general intelligence shall be characteristic of the people. They have no right to rest from toil, until every one of the three million slaves who groan upon our southern soil are free; until war, and the spirit of war are eradicated from the breast of man; until bloodshed and cruel oppression are done away. They have no right to cease from toil, until the thrones of tyrants are demolished; until aristocracies of blood, birth, and wealth are buried in one common grave. They have no right to rest until over all the earth the gospel has been preached and Christianity embraced — until

> ' The voice of singing,
>   Flows joyfully along:
> And hill and valley ringing
>   With one triumphant song,
> Proclaim the contest ended,
>   And Him who once was slain,
> Again to earth descended
>   In righteousness to reign."

III. By a manly submission to the govern-ment of God. There is a notion widely spread, that religion is an unmanly thing, that embracing it, be-trays a womanly weakness, that it is the product of superstitious fear, or of a fanatical imagination. Thousands who respect Christianity on account of its triumphs, who admire the Bible on account of the purity and sublimity of its doctrines, would lose the right hand, rather than be suspected of being tinc-tured with what are deemed the follies of Christians. Especially young men, shrink from having it known that they have any desire to become savingly inter-ested in the cross of Christ. On this rock thousands have shipwrecked salvation and their souls. Con-vinced of sin, of the need of a Saviour, they have hushed the voice of the Spirit — crushed the aspira-tions of the better nature, lest the world should place on them the brand of fanaticism ; and there are some present who would become submissive to the Divine will, and embrace humble piety, did they not deem the act childish and unfashionable. But how mistaken are such ! Pure religion instead of being childish, unmanly and weak, is honorable in the highest degree. God is our moral governor, and submission is honorable. God is our father, and obe-dience is honorable. God is our benefactor, and gratitude is honorable. You have earthly parents who have watched over your advancing years, who have protected you from childhood, and would shame tinge your cheek were it told that you revered and honored and obeyed those parents? No: and should a blush be seen, when God the Eternal Father is obeyed and worshipped? Religion consists in doing right, and is doing right, manly or unmanly? Religion is gratitude to a kind friend and benevolent benefactor, and is gratitude under such circumstances manly or unmanly? The angels are engaged night and day in the service of God — the highest intelligences of Heaven, bow before the dazzling throne with cease-less songs, and tell me, is such service manly or un-manly, honorable or dishonorable? Instead of be-ing a dishonorable work, the service of God is the highest and noblest which can engage the attention of angels or men; while sin is unmanly, weak, cow-ardly, debasing, and devilish. Every man who is converted and becomes a child of God has conferred upon him immortal glory, while every sinner who lives on in sin is covering himself with everlasting shame and disgrace. I am not alone in this view of the subject. Some of the mightiest minds have been found among those who have been believers in ex-perimental piety, and who have loved to attest by many works of love, their attachment to the reli-gion of the cross. Men from all professions — from all parties and all countries — from all ranks in life, and degrees of mental culture, have been found, who were not ashamed of Christ, but who deemed his religion manly and honorable. Sir Matthew Hale, one of the most distinguished Judges which England has ever had, *was a Christian.* Joseph Addison, one of the most beautiful writers of Europe, and who has added much to the literature of his native land, *was a Christian.* Cowper, Pollok, Milton, and other great poets of the world, *were Christians.* Fenelon, Mackintosh, Paley, Tillotson, Melancthon, *were Christians.* Sir Isaac Newton, one of the greatest philosophers who ever lived, and a host of others whose names I have no time to mention, *were Christians.*

Of our own countrymen some of the most illustrious have been among the professors of the faith of the cross, deeming it no reproach. The great leader of our tribes, Washington, was not only a godly man, but everywhere let it be known. The whole army, the officers and private members of the regiments, knew that he was a man of humble piety and prayer. Several of the framers of the declaration of independence were disciples of Christ, known and avowed. Several of our most able judges are men of like precious faith, and though of different creeds and sects, unite in their hearty attachment to vital godliness. The "old man eloquent," whose form we laid away as it were but yesterday, and whom the nation loveth to honor, was a man of piety. Amid the arduous duties which devolved upon him, he found time to commune with

3

God, and perform those duties which some of our
young men deem so childish and frivolous, but which
the venerable ex-President loved to perform, even to
his dying moment. These cases I select from a multitude of others which I only need time to produce,
as witnesses of the opinion, which these men of strong
minds and untarnished honor, have cherished in regard to the Christian faith.

And if it was not dishonorable to them, will it be
so to us? If they were called disciples, and the
charge brought no blush to the cheek, shall we be
ashamed of God our Father —of Christ our Saviour?

> "Ashamed of Jesus, sooner far,
> Let evening blush to own a star."

I have done. The time allotted for a single lecture has already expired, and what effect has been
produced ?   Have I aroused one manly feeling,
have I awakened one generous emotion, have I
kindled up in one mind a desire to do good, or
love God ?   Let thy heart be strong, young man, for
high and holy deeds, and be determined to be something more than a slave, who toils by day, and lies
down to sleep at night, forgetful of his kin, his country, and his God.

> "Count life by virtues — these will last
>   When life's lame-footed race is o'er;
> And these, when earthly joys are past,
>   Shall cheer us on a brighter shore."

LECTURE II.

YOUTH; ITS ADVANTAGES AND DISADVANTAGES.

Meditate upon these things; give thyself wholly to them; that thy profiting may appear to all. 1 *Timothy,* iv. 15.

THIS was part of an address delivered to a young man who was about to embark upon the sea of life, without experience and exposed to all the temptations by which the period of youth is surrounded. He had chosen a high and sacred calling. He had entered the Christian ministry, and had devoted himself to the work of reforming his fellow-men. Though commissioned by God and ordained by inspired men, he was yet to a considerable extent, to be the framer of his own course. His success as a man and as a minister, depended in a certain sense, upon the plan which he should pursue and the course of action which he should adopt. To guide him through the period of his inexperience, the apostle Paul directed to him the two epistles which bear his name. In these epistles certain sentiments are advanced, and certain principles of action prescribed, and the injunction is given, that he should meditate upon them, give them his serious consideration for the obvious reason, that his profiting might appear in his intercourse with men.

Those of us who are young are starting upon the voyage of life, more or less elated with hopes and prospects of success. With us, the period of childhood has passed away, and with it, the period of dependence upon parental oversight. Like a vessel which has left its moorings in the harbor, and stretched its canvas for a returnless voyage, and floated out upon the heaving bosom of the great ocean, so each young man has left the home of his childhood, the roof which sheltered him in infancy, and the scenes which clustered around him there, and gone forth to grapple with the stern realities of mature life. He may have kind parents and prudent friends, but they follow him not, and to a certain extent he is alone upon the world's wide waste. This is felt by every young person, as he goes forth into life to seek his own fortune, and carve out his own destiny. He enters his profession, locates himself in business, and feels that the great world is before him. In most cases high hopes are cherished. A fortune dazzles the eyes of the youthful aspirant, and he rushes on to secure it, without one single thought of failure. Most young men when they enter the active scenes of life appear to have made provision for nothing but complete and triumphant success. Whatever may be the object of pursuit, they seem to have it in their grasp, and in a multitude of cases meet nothing but misfortune and disappointment. You have seen the noble vessel leaving some. one of our harbors on the coast, on a beautiful morning in summer, with all sails spread, with every banner and pennant flying, with joy on every countenance and high hope beating in every heart. You have watched her progress as she walked through " the waters like a thing of life," and faded from your view upon the distant ocean. You have admired her majestic and imposing form, and wished yourself upon her deck, about to traverse with her, the fathomless deep. You have stood there long after she has disappeared from view, and have turned from the spot without dreaming that the noble vessel would become a wreck ere midnight. But follow her out to sea, and you will soon see dark clouds rolling over the sun — far away in the distance the hoarse thunder will mutter — the moaning sea will present a fearful aspect, and utter from her sepulchral lips ominous threatenings. Soon the storm will come. Peal after peal of thunder — flash after flash of lightning adds terror to the scene. The ship which you saw a few hours before, moving so majestically from the harbor will quiver upon the wave like the plaything of a child. The tattered sails, the falling masts, the broken helm, the wave-washed deck all present a frightful aspect. The billows swell high; like mountains they rise and fall with terrible fury upon the sinking vessel. In their terror the mari· ners pray to the God of the ocean and the storm for help. Lips long accustomed to blasphemy now utter supplications for mercy. But deaf to all their cries the storm rages on. One by one the unhappy men are swept away. Their last prayer mingled perhaps with the name of wife or child, rings out like a hollow wail over the deep, and all is hushed. The ship herself, unwilling to yield, struggles on a moment longer, and then with a terrible plunge descends to the bottom of ocean, and not one single object is left to mark the spot.

Such is the sad history of many of the most promising young men of our land. They commence life under the most flattering circumstances, but ere they have accomplished half the task, they are overtaken by storms of moral and commercial embarrassment, and are shipwrecked just where hope had painted the brightest vision of success. With this fact before me, I have concluded to present for your consideration this evening *a few themes for profitable meditation.* As the mariner starts upon his voyage, there are cer· tain facts and principles which he must keep before his mind. He must remember that storm is almost inevitable, and must be prepared to guard against it.

If he allows it to overtake him while he has all sail spread, and every sheet of canvas out, he must expect shipwreck. He will perhaps be becalmed, and against such an emergency must have a sufficient supply of bread and water. He is liable to be over-taken by piratical crafts, and hence must be ready for a conflict with them. If he goes forth thoughtless of all these considerations, his voyage will most certainly prove unsuccessful, his ship will founder in mid ocean, and the morning wave will sweep back to the city of his birth to tell his wife that she is a widow.

There are certain facts which all young men should remember as they commence the active duties of life. Remembered and acted upon, they will prove like the forethought of the mariner, and prevent the destruction of their enterprises. Forgotten, they will lead to the most disastrous consequences, and a want of the knowledge which these principles afford, will prove a source of misfortune and disappointment. You will allow me therefore to enumerate a few points on which we may do well to meditate, that our profiting may appear to all men.

I. YOUTH IS THE PERIOD WHEN THE CHARACTER IS FORMED. This is universally true. I am not prepared to admit that there is a single exception. All past experience testifies that in youth the man is moulded, and the bent given to his character. Even in those cases where the young man grows up virtuous and respected, and at thirty or forty years of age becomes corrupted and debased, we shall find if we rigidly examine his early history, that in his youthful days the foundation of a vicious character was laid, but in consequence of the peculiar circumstances under which he was placed, that character was not developed. This is the testimony of many who have died upon the scaffold. They have stated that the basis of their horrid crimes was laid perhaps in childhood, or in youth, but being surrounded by virtuous friends, the evil passions were restrained, but continued pent up in the bosom like the fires of a volcano. When years had rolled away, and there was less desire and inducement to keep the favor of society, these passions like the fires of heated Vesuvius, sent out their dreadful streams of moral destruction. On the other hand you find many who in their younger days were vicious, whose youth was stained with crime; but who as years rolled away reformed from vice and became useful members of society. A careless observer of human nature would suppose that reformation was the result of the thought and reflection of years, that as the mind became more mature, it became dissatisfied with the follies and crimes of youth. But in a majority, and perhaps I may say in all these cases, this is not the fact. Reformation instead of being the result of the experience and observation and reflection of years, may be traced back to childhood, to some isolated circumstance in youth, to the counsel of some Sabbath-school teacher, to the prayer of a dying father, to the exhortation written upon the blank leaf of the Bible by a sainted mother, or to something else which years of crime have been unable to efface from the memory. To illustrate this point a few cases will suffice. The character of Napoleon Bonaparte was formed in youth. His weak but ambitious friends taught him that he would at one day be a great conqueror. To inspire him with the same feelings, they formed mimic armies, and set him at the head of them, gave him a love of conquest and predominance, and thus laid the basis of his future character. Had the same care and expense been used to make of him a different being, the world would never have been astonished by his deeds of blood and crime. He might have been a Luther, a Howard, a Wilberforce, but for this unfortunate direction of his youth. The plays of his childhood made him the ambitious tyrant, and sent him like a scourge across the continent of Europe. Hume was a sceptic. It is said that in his early years he was a devout and conscientious believer in the word of God, but while young was in some debating association appointed to bring forward for sake of controversy, the arguments of the infidel. He consented. He studied long, brought his acute mind into contact with the sophistry of sceptics, and ere he was aware of it, had embraced their notions. Like melted lava his mind received sceptical impressions, and then con-gealed, and his whole after life bore the deformed and sightless image of infidelity. It is said of Vol-taire, one of the most brilliant writers of his age, that when five years old he committed to memory an in-fidel poem, and was never able after that to undo its pernicious influence upon his mind. He lived and died a corrupter of the world, and thousands who have been ruined by him will bewail his memory to all eternity.

It is said of one of the regicides who condemned to death the unfortunate Charles Stuart, king of England, that in early life he was of immoral charac-ter, but when about ten years of age he was passing a church in London, and stood at the door a-while to listen. He heard distinctly only one sentence, "If any man love not the Lord Jesus Christ, let him be Anathema Maranatha." He passed on to the com-mission of crime, but that fearful sentence followed him everywhere. At the age of twenty, it had pro-duced such an impression upon him that he deter-mined to reform, and became a man of influence and virtue. After the fall of Cromwell and the restoration of the crown, he fled to another country, and there when nearly eighty years of age, that single sentence weighed upon his mind and induced him to become a believer in Christ, as well as a man of virtue.   This same sentiment will be illustrated in the lives of all of us.   As young men we are forming characters and habits which will affect our old age, and make us virtuous or vicious, happy or miserable, in life's decline. I think I hazard nothing in saying that but few characters change materially after the age of twenty-five or thirty.   By that period habits become fixed, impressions formed, and the future character of the man made.   Nor is there so wide a difference in the minds of the young, as many seem to suppose.   There are not those towering distinctions at birth, which in after years make some intellectual wonders, and assign others to ignorance and degradation.   Though a natural difference of mind does undoubtedly exist, yet I apprehend that early impressions, and the discipline of youth, go further to make men intellectual giants or pigmies, than any original endowment of mind. The bearing of these remarks and illustrations upon young men will be plainly seen.   If character is formed in youth, then it follows that we are moulding our future lives, and by every act, writing out our own history.   If we form correct, virtuous, and manly habits, they will follow us to our graves, they will mark us through all our earthly course, and be the ornaments which shall deck our declining years. Look among the aged, and you will find various characters; the vicious and the virtuous, and if you search

out the history of each, you will find that age corre
sponds with youth. The miser was miserly when he
was young. The aged gambler commenced gambling
in some form when he was young. The drunkard
learned the vice in his youth. The hoary thief was
a dishonest boy. The sceptic drank in the poison of
his infidelity in early life. On the other hand, you
will find that the virtuous, laid the basis of that virtue
in years long since gone by. The lover of inspiration learned it on his mother's knee, or around the
family altar. The respecter of God, learned it ere
this deceitful world had marked its images of sin and
woe upon the soul, as deeply as in mature years.
Ask Philip Doddridge where he obtained the elements
of his noble character ? and he will tell you the story
of his mother, teaching him to love God by sentences
written on the tiles which composed the hearthstone.
Ask Richard Baxter where he obtained his character ?
and he will tell you of the efforts made by his father
upon his youthful mind and heart. Go to a host of
others and ask the same question, and they will point
back through years of sin and sorrow to youth or
early manhood. Scripture, nature, history, are all
full of the same sentiment, and in their various
ways inculcate the same truth. They alike declare that age is unbending as the forest oak, while
youth is as pliable as the tender sapling — that
age is as insensible to new impressions as the har-

dened rock, while youth is as yielding as the undried clay.

> A pebble on the streamlet scant,
>   Has turned the course of many a river;
> A dewdrop on the baby plant,
>   Has warped the giant oak forever."

Hence if we would form right characters ourselves, or help others to form right characters, we must begin before the middle of life. We must take the sapling ere it becomes a gnarled and tangled oak; we must take the little rivulet ere it has become swollen to a mighty river; we must take the clay ere it has been hardened into flinty rock, and rendered insensible to impressions.

II. YOUTH IS A SEASON OF GREAT ARDOR, GREAT FOLLY, AND GREAT MISTAKES. The ardor of youth is proverbial. Scarcely a young man can be found whose heart does not beat with high hopes, and whose bosom does not thrill with strong emotions. So short has been their acquaintance with the world, that they have not learned how deceitful are its pleasures, and how vain its pursuits. Hence they are flattered by every prospect, and engage in the various employments of life with the whole heart and strength. Old men distrust the world, they have been cheated by its hollow promises so many times, that they have become cautious and prudent. Not so with the young. If you will look over community you will find that those who are pushing into every hazardous enterprise, who are concocting schemes for reforming or deforming men, who embrace the wild and extravagant theories which are abroad, are drawn mostly from the young and inexperienced portion of society. Old men love the past, and live in it. Young men live in the future. Progress is their watchword, and they move onward, whatever may be before them. Our fathers respect venerable institutions, and have no desire for change. Their sons look with contempt upon the past, and regard nothing on account of its antiquity. The old way of living is tedious and irksome, and men live faster, move faster, think faster than in former times. Old men are content with doing a reasonable business; young men need a California to make them rich in a single hour. Our old men are willing to live in comfortable habitations in the quiet village; our young men talk of revelling in the halls of the Montezumas. Our old men are willing to study to be wise, and have made life a college course; our young men are ground out through intellectual mills, into the hopper of which the dunce and the prodigy go together. Our old men are content to live at home and practise life's stern duties; our young men talk of travel. They wish to stand on the Alps, or dig into the ruins of Herculaneum and Pompeii. They must walk the blood-stained streets of Paris — traverse the lanes and avenues of London, or mingle with the Italian throng as they crowd the streets of Rome. Our old men were willing to work for the bread they ate, and the cup of milk which they drank when weary; our young men have made servants of iron, and fire, and water, and converted them into curious combinations, to perform labor once done by human hands. These different changes have been effected by the restless activity of the young. The earnestness of youth is devoted to improvement, and the changes which we see, are the results of that earnestness. Nor would we have it otherwise. Improvement is the order of life, progress the law of society, and God has wisely placed old men and young men in the world together, that the young might drag the car of reformation, while the aged guide and control it.

But while the energy of young men suggests so many improvements in society, it also leads to many mistakes and follies. They who rush forward at every call, heedless of consequences; who stand in front of every battle; who are earnest for every new theory, will be liable to meet with disaster and defeat. The locomotive on the rail road, which has the heaviest press of steam, will perform the journey in the shortest time, and will also be more liable to leap from the track, and dash itself and the train which follows it, into ruin. The liability to disaster is proportionate to the pressure of steam. The mail-steamer in crossing the ocean will be likely to make a quicker passage, if she builds her fires hotter, and crowds her sails, and generates her steam more liberally; and she will also be more likely to meet with accident, and go to the bottom of the ocean. The danger is commensurate with the extraordinary speed. Thus is it, to some extent, with the energy of youth. While confined to certain limits, and flowing in a proper channel, it will secure the desirable result. But the more haste we make to be rich, the more eagerly we grasp for fame, the more zealous we are in any cause, the more liable are we to overstep the limits of prudence, and fall into fatal errors.

And thus has it been in all the history of the past. The enthusiasm of youth has led many into sad mistakes, and these mistakes have ended in the complete overthrow of the most brilliant schemes. How many young men have commenced business with the laudable purpose of supporting themselves. Before them the road to fortune was open, and they entered it. One speculation after another presented itself, one plan after another was adopted. Day by day, and week by week, they ventured into deeper water, and took upon themselves new obligations. Soon, instead of finding themselves the possessors of a fortune, they were bankrupt, and perhaps with the loss of money, came also the loss of credit and character. The tide of life is dotted with the wrecks of character, with the ruins of young men who started fair and with high prospects of usefulness, but who have failed, signally and fearfully failed. And why have they failed? Simply because they refused to profit by the experience of those who have preceded them, and have allowed the zeal of youth to trample upon reason, and blind the judgment and the conscience. A majority of the failures which are made by our young men might be avoided, would they heed the injunction of Paul, and meditate upon these things, which so intimately concern their success in this life, and their happiness beyond it. They who rush out into life determined to pluck its flowers, must look and see where they grow. If they bloom upon the border of some dark precipice, they must tread cautiously, lest they stumble in the attempt to secure the prize. If some venomous serpent lies coiled up at the root, they must be careful lest the hand which plucks the flower should be bitten by the viper.

III. YOUTH IS A PERIOD OF GREAT EFFORTS AND GREAT RESULTS. There has existed a notion in time past, that age alone was capable of performing great deeds, and accomplishing vast results. This notion has become to a great extent, a common sentiment, and we are apt to pass by young men, and deem them unworthy of notice, because their heads are not covered with silver locks, and their limbs trembling on the borders of the grave. I admit that age has the most experience, that old men are likely to act with more prudence and caution, but I also contend that youth may put forth efforts, and lead to great results. The history of the world has proved, that the young are better fitted for active or laborious service, than are their fathers, and in every enterprise where labor is required, we naturally look to young men. Our hostile armies are composed, to a considerable extent, of young men ; our most distinguished writers and statesmen, commenced in early life ; our poets and orators earned some of their freshest laurels while in the morning of their days.

From a work* published a few years since, I have gathered a few facts bearing upon this very point — facts which clearly illustrate my position, and prove that youth is capable of great deeds, and if properly improved will accomplish vast results. "It is said that one of the greatest military men of the world, Alexander the Great, was less than *thirty-three* years old when he subdued his enemies in Greece, took possession of the neighboring countries, passed into Asia, conquered the whole of Asia Minor, Syria, Egypt, and Persia, besides countless smaller kingdoms and a large part of·India." "Hannibal, who was the most formidable enemy which Rome ever had, was made General at the age of *twenty-two.* By the time he was *twenty-eight*, he

* Patton's Lectures to Young Men.

had driven the Romans from Spain and Gaul, had crossed the Alps with an immense army, and by the battle of Canae, had brought Rome itself into danger of capture." "Bonaparte, at the age *twenty-seven*, was made General of the French armies ; after which he subdued the whole of Italy, passed into Egypt, was made First Consul at the age of *thirty*, and having like Hannibal crossed the Alps, and by the decisive victory of Marengo again subdued Italy, was eventually crowned Emperor, having gained some of his most brilliant victories by the time he had reached the age of *thirty-five.*" "Hernando Cortes, the conqueror of Mexico, pushed his way up from obscurity, became commander of the expedition to Mexico, and by consummate boldness and unmitigated villany, became at the age of *thirty-five*, the master of the Aztec Empire." "If we turn to literary men, poets, orators and philosophers, we find Burke laying the foundation of his reputation for eloquence as a writer and speaker, as early as his *twenty-seventh* year, and composing his celebrated treatise on the 'Sublime and Beautiful,' in his *twenty-eighth* year." "Lord Bacon at the age of *sixteen* had conceived the design of overthrowing the philosophy of Aristotle, and at that early period in his life had openly expressed and promulgated his opposing views." "Sir Isaac Newton had made his most important discoveries in astronomy and mathematics, before he had reached the age of *thirty*."   "The younger Pitt be came Chancellor of the Exchequer, and Prime Minister of England, at the early age of *twenty-four*, and for many years conducted with consummate ability the complicated affairs of that great nation."   "Lord Byron published many of his choicest poems at the age of *thirty*."   "Burns gave to the public some of his most exquisite compositions at the age of *twenty-seven*."

"Among theologians we are struck with the fact that Calvin composed his celebrated 'Institutes,' when he was but *twenty-five* years of age."   "Philip Melancthon is a yet more wonderful instance of what can be accomplished in the early period of life.   At twelve years of age he went to the University of Heidelberg, and at fourteen was made Bachelor of Arts.   At *seventeen*, he was made Doctor of Philosophy.   At *twenty-one*, he was appointed Professor of Ancient Languages in the University of Wittemberg. While but a lad, he distinguished himself, and won the praise of Germany and the world."   "Alexander Pope, before he was *twenty-five*, had written many of his best poems."   "Dr. Dwight commenced the 'Conquest of Canaan,' when he was but *sixteen*, and completed it at the age of *twenty-three*."   To these cases might be added a multitude of others, and among them, many drawn from the history of our own country.   Eight of the men who signed the declaration of independence, and gave to the world that noble document, were under *thirty-five* years of age. Lafayette was but *eighteen* when he stood shoulder to shoulder with some of the most distinguished officers in the American army, and at the age of *twenty-four*, led on the National Guards of France. Washington was but a lad when he was entrusted with important offices, and some of his most distinguished battles were fought in his early youth. John Quincy Adams, at the age of *fourteen*, was private secretary to the Minister Plenipotentiary to the Court of St. Petersburgh. From this time, until he was chosen president, he continued to receive the most brilliant offices which the government could bestow, and furnishes us with a remarkable instance of what may be accomplished in one's early days. He performed more in boyhood, than most men accomplish in a long life of active service.

I refer to these cases as illustrations of the truth of the statement, that youth is capable of great results, and is distinguished for great deeds as well as for great follies and crimes. They also prove, that all which has been done to reform the world or enlighten it, or make it wiser, has not been done by age alone, but that youth has had its share in the improvement and adornment of mankind. If we should take from the world what has been done by young men, literature and science would be divested of half their beauty, and history would lose half the brilliant

deeds which it now records with triumph and satisfaction.

Thoughts like these, my readers, we should re
member. If there is one sin to which youth is
more addicted than another, if there is one fault to
which young men are exposed more than another, it
is the fault, the sin of thoughtlessness. There is a
haste, a precipitancy in the movements of the young,
which not unfrequently involves in ruin the fairest
prospect of success in life. The apostle Paul who
had seen more of life than his young disciple, Timothy, knew this, and urged him to *meditate* upon things
pure and excellent, that his profiting might appear to
all. The same caution is needed by the young men
of the present age, and unless they heed it, they will
place in jeopardy the dearest interests which they
cherish. But few of the sins of youth are committed
deliberately. The young man does not often deliberately and thoughtfully strike the blow which commits
him to the dungeon, or brings him to the scaffold —
he does not deliberately enter into schemes to ruin
others, by involving them in pecuniary or moral embarrassment — he does not often wilfully and maliciously enter any path of crime. But ere he is aware,
he is drawn step by step to such a distance from the
path of virtue, that the passage of return is hedged
up, the way back rendered impassable, and he goes
on to and maliciously and designingly what he com

menced thoughtlessly. Did men think more, how many a hand would be held back from crime ; how many lips would be sealed from perjury ; how many feet would turn away from the gates of hell. You have seen the sun as he arose in the east, and dissipated the clouds which impeded his way — you have seen that sun struggle through the mists of morning, a bright and shining luminary, and rise higher and higher in his heavenly progress, until the eye of the eagle was unable to withstand his gaze ; you have seen that sun high in the heavens, scattering his beams upon man below, and riding in his cloudy chariot crowned with fire, the acknowledged king of day. You have also seen a comet, a strange erratic thing, seemingly controlled by no law, subject to no government, flaming through heaven, dazzling the world for awhile, and then passing away in darkness. Like that sun we may commence in the morning of life, our steady onward progress, governed by laws of nature and of God ; we may progress in life, each year excelling the past in virtue, in happiness, in holiness, in usefulness. Like that sun moving on in an undeviating course, obeying with all precision the principles which control its progress, we may move on governed by laws as certain, and better understood ; until our path shall be like the path of the just, which shineth brighter and brighter unto the perfect day. Or we may be like the comet, dashing from its course, and setting worlds on fire. Like the comet we may obscure ourselves as soon, and as suddenly. By turning from the path of virtue and true honor, by leaving the great principles which God has laid down in his word, we shall be nothing but wrecked and ruined spirits. Meditate on these things, while life is young and buoyant, and thy sun shines fair. Be virtuous, be good, be circumspect, and no weapon formed against thee shall prosper.

> " Virtue may be assailed, but never hurt;
> Surprised by unjust force, but not enthrall'd;
> And even that which mischief meant most harm,
> Shall in the happy trial prove most glory."

LECTURE III.

So run that ye may obtain. 1 *Corinthians*, ix. 34.

EFERENCE is had in this passage, and in others of a similar character, which are scattered through the writings of the apostle Paul, to the foot races of the ancients. In the Olympic games, foot-racing seems to have been one of the most honorable and one of the most common. Men in high rank, and men in low rank, were accustomed in these exercises to contend for the prize, and he who was successful was wreathed with laurels, and received the praises, and almost the homage of the people. As the competitors ran in the race-course, they were cheered by the assembled multitude, and the victor deemed himself raised to the highest pinnacle of earthly fame. Paul in the text is exhorting the Corinthian Christians to run the spiritual race, and earnestly contend for the spiritual prize. He urges them not to run for a corruptible crown, a fading laurel, or a transitory breath of applause ; but for an incorruptible crown, an unfading laurel, an imperishable glory. He wishes them to imitate the conduct of the ambitious racers, as they press on to secure the reward set before them, and be as zealous to run the Christian race, as were they to receive a cluster of evergreens, and the shouts of an excited multitude.

Human life may well be compared to a race-course, in which a countless number of persons are contending for the prize. The aged have nearly finished — the young have just commenced. The prize set before them is success, which most persons suppose to be a competent support, an unsullied reputation, and a useful life. And indeed if we confine ourselves to the present life, and leave out the future, we find that these are the chief elements of prosperity, which it is the duty as well as the right of the young man to secure if possible. But in order to secure prosperity and success in this life, care must be taken and effort put forth. It is not every aspirant for wealth, fame, and pleasure, that will secure them. It is a race in which hundreds and thousands are disappointed at every trial, and where one succeeds, and receives the wreath of victory, many others tire and faint ere half the course is finished. In the Olympic games, the racers were required to make extensive preparation for the trial. For ten whole months they were accustomed to exercise themselves, and were trained by different masters, to all those exercises which were calculated to give strength and vigor to the body.   Their diet was strictly regulated, and during a part of the time, their only food consisted of dried figs, nuts, and other similar fruits.   When they entered the race, they were required to lay aside all unnecessary clothing, and divest themselves of everything which could impede their progress, or prevent their running with the greatest speed.

For the race of life, preparation will be needed. The young man who enters it, and is bent on securing success, will find that one path, and one alone, leads to it; that all the other avenues and lanes of life, though apparently parallel, are leading in different directions, and are filled with pitfalls and dangers; that there is but one star which guides the traveller through it, while all other lights are as deceptive as the *ignis fatuus*, which plays with phosphoric beauty over marshy grounds, upon which if the foot of man shall tread he will be placed in fearful jeopardy.   He will find that life is no rail road, along which we are borne without toil or effort, on cushioned seats or downy pillows; that life's great employment does not consist in plucking flowers and listening to sweet music.   He will find life to be a race, a contest not of whistling locomotives, not of white-winged ships, but of toiling men, on foot, shoulder to shoulder, struggling for the prize. With this view of human life, I proceed to enumerate SOME OF THE SOURCES OF SUCCESS.

I. INDUSTRY. It is a law of God, an ordinance of Heaven, that man shall work. It is a fixed principle, a certain law, that in the sweat of the brow shall the bread be eaten. There is no law which specifies a man's employment, or assigns him to this or that post of toil. There is no arrangement of God by which one is to cultivate the earth, and another to manufacture our garments and construct our dwellings. He has in no way, other than by the arrangement of his providence, made one man the producer, and another the distributor of his bounty. But he has made labor and toil essential to success in life, and has sent his decree to all nations, that he who worketh not, shall not eat. I am aware that sometimes a fortune is made in a single day; that by some turn of the wheel, a poor man is made unexpectedly rich, and raised at once from poverty to affluence. But such fortunes are exceptions to the ordinary course of events, and as a general thing, become a curse to those who inherit them, or to their children. The ideas which men cherish of becoming rich in a moment, of making a fortune by a ticket in the lottery by a throw of dice, by a commercial speculation, are all chimerical. God has ordained it otherwise, and though by these methods, money in immense

sums, is sometimes obtained, yet it goes as easily as
it comes. The only path to wealth in which the young
man can travel with safety is *industry*. The only
way in which he can build up a fortune worth possessing, is by toil — the toil of years. Deluded and deceived by phantom appearances, the farmer is often
induced to leave his plough, the mechanic his workshop, the tradesman his store, and the student his
books, to embark in some wild chase for wealth, some
erratic scheme for gaining the smiles of the god of gold,
instead of being content to plod along in the old way,
adding, month by month, to the increasing fund deposited in the bank or invested in stocks. Some brilliant chance is presented, by which if things work
well, the hundred dollars which is on deposit, may be
turned into a thousand. Filled with the hope of being
rich at once, the little sum which has been earned by
hard service, is invested, the note of the speculator is
taken, and the dupe begins to dream of high houses,
broad lands, swift horses — *all his own*. Months roll
on, and he finds that the scheme was all the deception of a villain, and the little treasure which was
placed in his hands is gone. If you will glance at
the lives of those men who have amassed large fortunes, who have been eminently successful in commercial projects, you will find them to be men of correct
business habits, and of unwonted effort. You will
find that they have arisen early in the morning, that

they have worked hard during the day, and remained up late at night. Their minds and hands have been busy, their whole attention has been given to the object of their pursuit, and they have been successful. Had they in early years substituted hazard and specu lation for hard work, they would have failed of secur ing the object of their desires. Had they been de luded by some gold-mine monomania, and left their families and homes, and gone forth across mountains and rivers and plains, amid wild beasts and fiercer men, to dig for the shining ore, they would have dug into their own graves. Had they listened to the voice of every wild-brained moneymaker, their for tune would have consisted only of the notes of bank rupt speculators. Had they tried the gaming-table, they might also have tried the penitentiary and the prison.

I know there is a charm about this speedy way of making money, but it should be resisted. The young man goes into the bowling-alley, the gaming-saloon, and sits down there to see the sport. In a moment one of the players becomes the winner, and scrapes the shin ing gold at once into his pocket. "How easily this is done," exclaims the novice. "Here I have toiled hard to earn ten shillings during the day, and this man has made ten dollars in a single hour." He feels for his purse, and finds in it a little money which he was reserving for his wife and child at home. He

sits down to play. He wins. Twice, thrice, he wins.
He runs away to the savings-bank, where he has laid
up a few hundred dollars. All the way he dreams
of gold — a fortune. The gambling-room seems full
of money. How rich he will be to-morrow! His
wife shall now live in splendor — his child shall be
orought up in luxury. With one dollar he won ten,
and with his hundreds he may win thousands. Thus
speculating he returns to the gay saloon. The
sharpers see him come, and wink at one another.
They know that the earnings of years are in his
purse, and their code of honor requires its transfer to
their pockets. The foolish one sits down among them,
and the game commences. They urge him to drink.
He never used wine before, but it will sharpen his
wits now, and he drains the cup. The game excites
him. He wins and loses — loses and wins. At midnight he thinks of returning to his home, but on
counting his money, he finds that on the whole, he
has been a loser. He has twenty or fifty dollars less
than when he commenced. He must win that back
again. Again they gather around the table closer
than before, and our hero is more mad than ever.
He has become reckless. He stakes his all, and
loses. The toil of years is gone. Excited, maddened, infuriated, drunk, he rushes from the fatal spot, a
ruined man. With bloodshot eyes, and haggard
look, he returns to his family, and changes his home

from paradise to perdition. His haste to be rich has destroyed him.

Nor can *a good reputation* be earned in an hour. Those men who have secured the respect and esteem of the world, as philosophers, statesmen, and philan-thropists, have not done it by one single act, or by any short series of acts, but by patient and persever-ing industry. They have added virtue to virtue, one element of knowledge to another, and by degrees laid the basis of a valuable character. And thus must it be with the young men whom I address to-night. If they would be successful in life, if they would acquire property, secure the respect of mankind, and be use-ful while they live, they must do it by the patient and persevering industry of years. Instead then of de-vising schemes for sudden aggrandizement, go to work in your calling, whatever it may be, lose but few half-days, and avoid all those military and civic societies which are forever laying assessments. Be punctual to all your appointments. Make it a prin-ciple never to be left by the cars or the stage-coach, never too late at the table, in the workshop, or in the family. Fortunes and characters are sometimes lost by a want of punctuality, and one of the most disagreeable and unprofitable habits which we can form, is, to be *always late*. A distinguished man in a neighboring State, a man of wealth and influence, was asked, how he secured so large a fortune in so few years? Without giving a direct reply, he said: "I was never late at an appointment, or behind my time, in my life."

Whatever your business may be, *persevere in it.* Do not be a mechanic to-day, and a trader to-morrow — a lawyer to-day, and a minister next week — a school-master now, and a physician soon. "He who has learned all trades is good at none," and he who is driving from one employment to another, will generally fail in all. The chimney-sweep with his black face and sooty blanket, will become a richer man than one who stays in one branch of business only until he can find another.

Remember, too, that industry is honorable, and idleness disgraceful. The rich man, the possessor of millions, who allows his wealth to purchase for him exemption from toil, is a disgrace to his race. He forfeits not only his claim to his fortune, but to his character, and should be regarded as one of the *drones* which society is compelled to drag along with it. The notion which prevails extensively in Europe, and in our southern States, and to some extent, in enlightened and beloved New England, that labor is disgraceful, is a false notion, and should receive the contempt of all men. The green-jacket of the mason, or the carpenter, besmeared with lime, or covered with dust, is as honorable as the broadcloth of the merchant whose ships are in every port. The black-

5

smith's hammer is as honorable as the sheriff's staff. The busy hum of labor, is as eloquent as the plea of the lawyer, or the charge of the judge. And so all those men who have been truly great have regarded it. Washington was not ashamed to acknowledge himself a farmer, and when his services were required by his country, he went from his field to the presidency, and when he had accomplished his mission, he retired to his toil again. A large majority of the men who have been members of Congress, have been hard-working, industrious farmers and mechanics, who have been selected by the people, as best adapted to aid in the councils of the nation. The best and greatest men we have, are found to be those who regard labor as an honor rather than a crime. An amusing anecdote is related of Prof. Stuart, one of the best scholars of the age, which illustrates his opinion of that class of men who despise toil, and seek to avoid it: "A student from one of the southern States, in the Theological Seminary at Andover, had purchased some wood and was exceedingly embarrassed at being unable readily to obtain some one to saw it for him. He went to Prof. Stuart, to inquire what he should do in such an unfortunate predicament. The learned professor replied, that he was out of a job himself, and he would saw it for him." *

II. FRUGALITY. If there is a contemptible man

* Arvine's Cyclopædia

on earth, one who seems to have lost sight of the true design of life, one who has no idea of true enjoyment, it is the avaricious miser. It is a sad sight to see a human being, whose spirit will soon stand before God, and whose body will erelong crumble back to dust and ashes, heaping up gold, only that he may hide it from every gaze but his own, that he may count it over and over, and dream about it at night, and gloat over it by day, *and die.* It is also disgusting to see a man, who if he does not go to such an extreme, seems desirous of keeping all he gets, refusing the calls of benevolence, denying the claims of nature, that he may retain what he by honesty or dishonesty, may have secured. But if avarice and covetousness are to be condemned, so are extravagance and prodigality. There are many young men in the country, who practise no economy in their pecuniary transactions. While they have money, it goes with a lavish hand. The present moment, they provide for, and leave the future to care for itself. It matters not whether their income is three hundred or three thousand dollars, they spend it all, and until they come to the bottom of the purse, they live high and fast. I think I may be allowed to say that extravagance is one of the sins of youth. In the desire which young men have to avoid a mean, niggardly spirit, they are apt to lean to the side of prodigality, and become spendthrifts. This is the reason why we find so few men who are in possession of any considerable amount of property. Every desire must be gratified, every wish complied with, and thus thousands are kept poor, who otherwise would be in independent circumstances. Fortunes are squandered every year by those who in after life will look back with regret to the scenes of youth; squandered, too, to secure objects which are entirely worthless.

I will not, of course, specify the particulars in which economy may be practised. They will readily present themselves to your own minds, and if you will appeal to your past experience, short as it may have been, you will find it confirming my statement. True, the amount spent daily in the purchase of useless things is small. When looked at by itself, it seems an insignificant sum; but multiply it by the days in the year, and the number of years of life, and it is magnified to a competency, which no man would despise.

Beside the tendency of extravagance to poverty, it is the basis of many habits equally pernicious as itself. The prodigal knows not when . to stop. His own substance he wastes with riotous living, the portion which he inherits from father or mother, is scattered like the leaves before the blasts of Autumn, and unless his heart is doubly guarded against temptation, he will resort to fraud or forgery to maintain the position in society which his extravagance has purchased for him.   The income of most young men is small.   If they have many wants to gratify, that income will be insufficient for them, and some other source of revenue must be found. Those little "six cent" desires which accumulate so fast, are the ones which drive so many hundreds of young men to the gaming-table, and induce them to become worthless, idle, and dissipated.   Extravagance is the parent of many crimes, and has destroyed fortunes, blasted characters, and been to our young men the prolific source of evil and sorrow.   The records of bankruptcy, the gaming-table, the cell of the forger, the prison of the felon, are all eloquent upon this subject, and utter their mournful lessons of wisdom and experience,

> "Look round, the works of waste behold,
> Estates dismember'd, mortgag'd, sold!
> Their owners now to jails confin'd,
> Show equal poverty of mind."

III. TEMPERANCE.   Intemperance has long been a fearful scourge.   Though checked and controlled to some extent now, it is still making fearful ravages. Years ago almost all men were in the habit of using intoxicating liquors.   Through whole communities but few could be found, who had rigidly abstained from its use.   The farmer could not plough his field without it.   The mechanic could not hew his timber, or fashion his iron, without it.   The lawyer could not prepare his brief, the physician could not visit his patients without it. The minister could not preach without it, and doubtless many of the sermons of our old divines were written and delivered under its influence. It was used at the marriage festival, and in the chamber of mourning, in the halls of the living, and over the graves of the dead. It was the companion of solitude, and the friend of the crowded assembly; it held dominion in the house of God, and amid scenes of violence and disorder. But times have changed. Intemperance, open, reeling intemperance, has become disreputable and criminal, and we shrink from the example of the tattered inebriate as from the pestilence. But still intemperance in other forms, is almost as prevalent as in the days of our fathers. The wine-cup is circulated freely and fearlessly, and hundreds of young men are ruined by it annually. Now success in life is out of the question unless the wine-cup and the maddening bowl are totally abjured, unless rigid, consistent, manly temperance is made the rule of life. Drink tendeth to poverty, and bankruptcy; ruin, rags and misery are as sure to follow a course of intemperance, as is light to follow the rising of the sun.

I knew a young man, who three years since, was virtuous, loved, and respected. He had just established himself in business, and was exceedingly prosperous. He was often seen in the house of God, and around him a little family was congregated. His connections were respectable, and his prospects in life were quite propitious. He had an intelligent and lovely companion, whom he had taken from a home of wealth, refinement, and happiness. He had everything to make him comfortable, and lead him up to virtue and to God. But he loved his wine, and deemed it an innocent beverage. Hence he drank it, and became drunken. Step by step he descended the drunkard's pathway. Day by day he became more habituated to the fearful vice. Soon all restraint was gone, business was neglected, home deserted, family abused, confidence and reputation gone, and the once prosperous and respectable young man has now become an outcast and a vagabond. Month by month, I have seen the cheek of the wife grow pale, and lines of sorrow traced on her once happy countenance. Week by week I have seen her come bending to the sanctuary, to find solace here in the worship of her God. Day by day has she toiled to earn money and clothing to send to that husband who has deserted her, and whom she follows like a ministering angel. Three years have been sufficient to accomplish the whole, to blast the fondest hopes, to crush the highest aspiration, to shroud a family in ruin, to break the heart of a wife, to bring disgrace upon the child, to make the hair of the father grey with sorrow, (not with age), and send the unhappy cause of all this, along the streets, a howling, infuriated drunkard.

"Ah! drinking! drinking! bane of life,
Spring of tumult, source of strife,
Could we but half thy curses tell,
The world could wish thee safe in hell."

And yet with the fact before them, that intemperance is destructive to life, health, property, business, to all things good, many of our young men are bringing by the use of wine, ruin upon themselves and their families. Though the Golgotha of drunkenness is before their eyes, though all the past is pointing to the long army of inebriates who have perished in the march of time, yet they drain the cup, swallow " the beverage of hell," as though it was the water of life.

IV. HONESTY. This I conceive to be the crowning excellence of youth. An honest young man has in his bosom a treasure of more real value than the wealth of nations. Should I be asked, what would most contribute to a man's success, in any vocation whatever, I would reply: HONESTY. Should I be asked what would most certainly prevent success, I would reply: DISHONESTY. Now it occurs, that to dishonest practices, the young men of our land are particularly exposed. While females are protected from the temptations to this sin, while from the peculiarity of their situation in society, they are to a considerable extent secure, young men are surrounded with inducements and temptations. Just com-

mencing life, they wish to do well, and not unfre·
quently imagine, that to succeed they must make
money fast, and get rich quick, and hence to secure
this, will embark in many a scheme of doubtful char-
acter.   The expenses of poor young men are generally more than equal to their income, and if they are
bent on living extravagantly, they will be tempted to
enter into many a course of folly and crime to obtain
the necessary funds.   But however expert the dishonest man may be, however long he may go on un-
interrupted in his villany, however successful he may
be at the onset, he will assuredly fail.   The forger
cannot long continue that sin without. detection ; the
counterfeiter will assuredly be taken in his own snare ;
the gambler will come to poverty, and the thief
will bring himself to the prison and the dungeon.
There is no safety for a young man in the early period of life, without strict and unbending integrity in
word and deed.   Complete failure will sooner or later,
come upon every man who does not subscribe to the
principles of rectitude.   I know that dishonesty is
prevalent.   I know that it exists everywhere, and to
a fearful extent enters into all the affairs of life.   As
Shakspeare says :

> " To be honest, as this world goes,
> Is to be one picked out of ten thousand."

Not seldom is the clerk taught to inform the customer, that certain goods cost such a sum, that they are durable and fashionable, when he knows it to be false. Not seldom is the ignorance of the purchaser made the cause of a "good trade," and apprentices are led to look upon such a fraud as a harmless transaction. In these and a thousand other ways are the principles of honesty shamefully violated and outraged, and the basis is laid for a long and aggravated course of crime and duplicity. But the old maxim, "honesty is the best policy," will be found to be true in all the transactions of life. What though a man does make a momentary advance in his business by dishonesty? What though at the end of each year he is a hundred dollars richer than he would have been but for his fraud? What though he may have enlarged his store and beautified his residence, and secured the smiles of the wealthy? What though he is enabled to ride in his carriage, and dress in gilt and gold? Will not the vengeance of God follow him? Will not his ill-gotten gains rust and canker his heart? Will not commercial distress or some other element of destruction sweep away his property, taking the well-earned with the ill-gotten?

I knew a young man who started in life with high hopes and prospects. He had a little property to commence with, and was determined that it should increase at all hazard. Honestly or dishonestly, he was bound to be rich. His motto was, "All is right in trade," and well did he carry it out He thought

it was the duty of his customers to find out defects in the goods which they purchased of him;
they were the ones to discover what was bad in the
bargain. He supposed he was clear when he had
made the sale, and felt compelled by no principle of
morality to help his customers make good bargains.
Thus it continued awhile. He would openly boast
of having made this sum and that sum, from this and
that person. He seemed to be growing rich, his
place of business was crowded. His fair stories and
smooth looks, drew a crowd of visitors, and for awhile
he made money very rapidly. But the curse—God's
curse was on him and his business. When he least
expected it, a great failure in another city occurred,
the intelligence of which came upon him like a clap
of thunder in a cloudless day. Other failures followed, and he began to reap the reward of his dishonesty.
When he began to sink, reports of his dishonesty,
which until then had been hushed, spread like wild-
fire, and soon he found it impossible to continue
his business. Those who had money and goods were
afraid of him. Confidence in his character was gone,
and he was obliged to relinquish business entirely,
move from the fine house in which he lived, and
become a clerk, and was looked upon with suspicion
even at that. I have known other men in business,
who have met with disasters and failures, and have
stood unaffected by them, superior to their crushing

influence, from the simple fact that they were honest
men, and could look community in the face with a
consciousness that though they were unfortunate,
they were not guilty.   Thompson in his lectures to
young men, states the following fact, which to my
own mind, is of considerable interest.   "The late
president of the United States Bank, once dismissed
a private clerk, because the latter refused to write for
him on the Sabbath.   The young man, with a mother
dependent on his exertions, was thus thrown out of
employment, by what some would call an over-nice
scruple of conscience.   But a few days after, when
the President was requested to nominate a cashier for
another bank, he recommended this very individual,
mentioning this incident as a sufficient testimony to
his trustworthiness.   'You can trust him,' said he,
'for he would not work for me on the Sabbath.'"
Awhile since, a young man was dismissed from his
place, because he would not become party to a falsehood, by which refusal the firm failed to secure several hundred dollars which did not belong to them, but
which they expected to obtain.   For the crime of
honesty ana truth the young man was dismissed from
his position.   A few days afterwards hearing of a va-
cant situation, he applied for it.   The merchant who
wished for an accountant, asked if he could refer him
to any individual with whom he was known, and who
would recommend him as an upright young man

With conscious innocence, and firm in his uprightness, he replied, "I have just been dismissed from Mr. ———'s, of whom you may inquire. He has tried me, he has known me." When applied to, his former employer gave a full and free recommendation, and added, "He was too conscientious about little matters." The young man is now partner in a large firm in Boston, and is apparently becoming rich.

A multitude of cases might be added, illustrating the value of honesty, and the great danger and shame of falsehood and fraud. Business men will rehearse them to you by scores, and prove that under any circumstances, "honesty is the best policy." And so you, my young friends, will find it in all your dealings with your fellow-men, and as you grow older in life, the conviction will become stronger and deeper, that a good reputation for honesty and manliness is above all price.

> "The purest treasure mortal lives afford,
> Is spotless reputation; that away,
> Men are but gilded worms or painted clay."

Remember these things as you advance in life, my young brethren, and as you grow older preserve your integrity. Be above the little arts and tricks of small men, and if you grow rich, let it be by honest and patient industry. Build not up a fortune from the labors of others, from the unpaid debts of creditors, from the uncertain games of chance, but from manly effort which never goes unrewarded. Never engage in any business unless you can be honest in it; if it rill not give a fair living without fraud, leave it, as you would the gate of death. If after all, you are poor, if by exerting yourself nobly and manfully, if by living honestly and uprightly you cannot secure a competency, then submit to poverty, aye, to hard, grinding poverty. Be willing, if it must be so, to breast the cold tide of want and sorrow, see your flesh waste day by day, and your blood beat more heavily, than make yourself rich, at the expense of honesty.

There are other sources of success in life, which might be mentioned, but these four will suffice for the present discourse. If a young man is industrious, frugal, temperate, honest, he will also have many other valuable traits of character. These never go alone. They bring a countless host of virtues and blessings in their train. Remember also that it is not our whole object to become rich and happy here. We are immortal. There is a life beyond this — *a world to come.*

> "Oh! what is life? At best a brief delight,
> A sun, scarce bright'ning ere it sinks in night;
> A flower, at morning fresh, at noon decayed;
> A still, swift river, gliding into shade."

We know that delight will soon be gone; that sun

will set, perhaps in tears ; that flower will droop, wither and decay ; that river will flow on, until no human eye shall be able to trace its progress ; but the life of the soul continues, and is to be affected for weal or woe, for countless ages, by its narrow and limited stay on earth. How terrible, then, is man's mission ! how solemn his responsibilities ! how glorious his destiny !

> " 'Tis God's all-animating voice
>   That calls thee from on high;
> 'Tis his own hand presents the prize
>   To thine uplifted eye ; —
> That prize, with peerless glories bright,
>   Which shall new lustre boast,
> When victors' wreaths and monarchs' gems
>   Shall blend in common dust."

LECTURE IV.

To everything there is a season, and a time to every purpose under the heaven. *Ecclesiastes*, iii. 1.

ITH pride and exultation the votary of pleasure will often refer to the first few verses of the chapter, from which my text is taken, and draw from them an argument in favor of sin and folly. Is there not a time to laugh and a time to dance? Does not inspiration tell us, that mirth and cheerfulness are allowable, and that the sports of the world are proper? Have we not the example of men in all ages; not the profane and sinful merely, but the best and noblest of our race? These and kindred questions are put to us with triumph by the seekers of pleasure of all kinds, who profess to be acquainted with the chapter under consideration, if they are ignorant of all the other sacred writings. They seem to have made *this* their study, quote it with freedom, and seem wonderfully impressed with the truth of Scripture, when they can bring it to bear upon the pursuit of their worldly and carnal amusements, and plead the example of some of the wise and good men who have fallen into error.

But those who read with attention the works of Solomon, could never come to any such conclusion. Raised by God to the throne, he was surrounded with everything to make him happy. His kingdom was glorious, the fame of his administration spread over the world, and wealth poured its streams lavishly at his feet. Surrounded by life's brightest scenes, he sought awhile his pleasure in them, he builded houses, he planted vineyards, he obtained men-singers and women-singers, he had instruments of music, and in every possible way strove to satisfy the longings of his nature for happiness. Labor, wealth, skill, time, were not spared, but all contributed to the monarch's pleasure. Thus he lived awhile, until the whole head was sick, and the whole heart faint—until he was convinced that all the objects of his earthly pursuits had no abiding bliss, and he turned from them, exclaiming, "Vanity of vanities, all is vanity."

Nor will the declaration of the wise man, that there is "a time to dance," extenuate any of the sinful amusements of the present age. He no more intended to justify that debasing and ruinous system, which we have at present, than to justify mur-

6

der when he said, there is " a time to kill." The dancing of the ancients was a religious and healthy recreation. It had no resemblance to what we call dancing now. It was performed with pure and elevated motives, and had no tendency to debase the mind or pollute the heart. One writer, thinks that " it always was a religious exercise ; that dancing for amusement was sacrilege ; that men who diverted it from a sacred use were deemed infamous, and declares, that there are no instances upon record in the Bible of social dancing for amusement, except that of the vain fellows, void of shame, alluded to in Micah ; of the irreligious families described by Job, which produced increased impiety and ended in destruction ; and of Herodias, which terminated in the rash vow of Herod, and the death of John the Baptist." All the cases, except these, were on occasions of religious festivity. Dancing was merely a token of joy and gratitude to God. It generally followed great victories, and was attended with sacred songs, and the sound of many musical instruments. As men now clap their hands and shout when any gratifying event has transpired, so the ancients sang and danced over their victories. The two sexes never united in it ; men danced alone, and maidens danced alone. They crowded not into pent-up halls, they were not excited with wine, they were not impelled by passion, they were not moved by lust. The green earth was their festive hall, the bright sun was their chandelier, the golden flowers shed their fragrance, and nature's own temple gave back the echo of their glad songs. To compare the pure, chaste worship of the ancients, with the brutish dancing of the present time, and justify one by the other, is to cast dishonor upon God, and insult the memory of his worshippers.

The only object had in view by the monarch writer, seemed to be the promulgation of the sentiment, that for all things there is an appointed time ; that joy and sorrow, work and play, will come in their order, and each should be attended to in its proper place. He did not attempt to defend vice, or offer a plea for the indiscriminate pursuit of pleasure. All his writings abound with warnings and cautions, and utter loudly their remonstrance against every course of sin.

Without further introduction I will turn your attention to INNOCENT AMUSEMENTS, as the subject for consideration. I do not design to offer an apology for any of the vain amusements and seductions of the world, or lead you to look with less disapprobation upon the vices by which we are surrounded. Accursed they are, and accursed they will remain. The press may plead for them, the pulpit may apologize for them, and the whole country may be bent on their pursuit, but God's displeasure will follow them, and their votaries. I simply wish to offer a few thoughts on amusements, and show that the highest pleasures, are the pleasures of innocence, and that sinful amusements fail to accomplish their object. Hence I remark,

I. MEN NEED, AND WILL HAVE SOME KINDS OF RECREATION. The body was not made for constant toil, the mind was not formed for constant study. God has not ordained that life shall be spent in one continued series of efforts to secure the things of this world. He has fitted man for enjoyment, as well as labor, and made him susceptible of pleasurable emotions. He did not design him for a slave, to dig the earth awhile and die; to toil on until the hour of death comes to conduct a shattered system back to dust and ashes. On the other hand, he has given him a physical system which like the harp, may be touched to any tune. He has made the eye, the ear, the mouth, all inlets of pleasure. He has so constituted us, that we may be wound up to the highest degree of pleasure, and receive through the medium of the senses a flood of happiness. Besides this, he has arranged the outward world in such a manner, as to give man the highest enjoyment. Had God designed man for ceaseless labor, he would not have given him such a body as he now possesses, he would have darkened the eye, deadened the ear, and blunted all the nicer sensibilities, and made the hand as hard as iron, and the foot as insensible as brass. But formed for enjoyment, we find men seeking it. After the labor of the day is over, and the toil of life done, they turn to every quarter to find some source of recreation, some avenue of life which is fragrant with flowers and which echoes with sweet music. Now this desire for recreation instead of being quenched, should be controlled and directed; instead of being totally discouraged, it should be turned into pure and holy channels, and made to result in the good of man, and the glory of God. One great mistake made by the Puritans, arose from a desire to suppress all amusements, to quench in man the desire for mirth and recreation, to make youth as sedate and grave as age, the child as sober and solemn as the sire. Hence instead of making the *Sabbath* a day of holy rest and calm enjoyment, they made it a season of constraint and fear. Children, instead of loving to have its sacred hours arrive, and hailing them with gladness, looked forward to the day as one of tedious, irksome slavery, on which they would be required to engage in meaningless services, answer difficult questions, and sit the live-long day with folded hands, and downcast eyes They pursued the same course in relation to other things. Sinful amusements were strictly forbidden, and severely punished. By the pulpit and the press they were denounced, and yet no measures were taken to substitute innocent pleasures in their stead, or furnish panting youth with any reasonable source of relaxation. The conse quence was, the young chafed under these restraints awhile, and then broke over them, and rushed out into paths of folly and destruction.

Not unfrequently we hear parents lamenting that they cannot keep their children at home ; that they do not love home ; that very early in life they have a desire for the company of strangers, and as soon as they are old enough will wander away from the mother's prayer, and the father's counsel. But on investigation we generally find that such parents are, to a considerable extent, responsible for the conduct of their children. They have failed to make home what it ought to be. They have not made it attrac- tive and pleasant. They have not provided amusing and profitable books, and spread around the hearth- side those allurements which are necessary to engage the attention, and secure the presence of the young. It is impossible for us to love unlovely objects, and HOME cannot be loved, if the father's countenance wears a perpetual frown ; if the mother is fractious and childish ; if occasional disputes disturb the har- mony and prosperity of the circle ; if no book is found on the shelf ; if no kindly sympathies are felt and ex- pressed. The secret of saving children from destruc- tion consists to a great extent, *in making home lovely and attractive*, and did parents understand this secret they would not be called upon so frequently to bewail the conduct of prodigal sons, and mourn over the destruction of fallen daughters. A clergyman told me, a few days since, that he had a son, who, when quite a child manifested an uneasy and roving disposition. Home did not appear attractive, and on every occasion he would steal away to spend the evening in the company of strangers. Filled with anxiety, the father began to look about for a remedy. He watched his son, and endeavored to discover the bent of his inclination. He saw that the boy had a fondness for music, that he would visit those places where singers resorted, and where musical instruments could be found. He saw that he was most willing to visit those families where the piano was an article of parlor furniture, and where the violin or the harp made their melody. His course was founded on this discovery. He purchased at considerable expense an instrument of music, and spread through his parlor, note-books and songs, everything of that kind which the father's means would allow was furnished, and soon the son became as fond of home, as he had previously been of strangers. His talent was for music, but as he could not enjoy it at home, he searched for it where it was; but when music came to cheer his own dwelling, he had no occasion to leave the warm hearth-side of parental kindness. Were I speaking exclusively to parents, I would urge them, to make home happy, to keep all strife and bitterness away, and ever in the presence of children wear a contented and cheerful look. If you feast, let it be at home, and let children partake of the good things ; if you have newspapers in your family, have among the rest, one adapted to your children ; if the profound, logical work which you read yourself, lies upon the table, let one be beside it, adapted to your children. Make them think that no place on earth can compare with home, and as they grow older, find amusement and recreation for them. Be not afraid to hear them laugh, though the house rings. When they wish for sport, do not drive them out into the street, or into the house of a good-natured neighbor, but bear a little, and remember that *you* were once a child.

The same remarks are applicable to a whole community. If there are no seasons of reasonable and pure pleasure, the young will resort to enjoyments which are vicious and destructive. If the social circle, the literary lecture, the musical concert, the debating association, the circulating library are not found, the theatre, the gaming-table, the ball-room, the brothel, will have full success. The young man needs relaxation and change, he must have it, it is in accordance with the laws of his nature, and if he cannot find it in innocent, he will resort to sinful pleasures.

I am acquainted with a town which a few years ago was notorious for the variety and extent of its sinful amusements. Every evening the festive hall was lighted, theatrical performances were crowded with visitors, the strolling circus found ready access, and the curse of God seemed to have settled on the place. Pure religion died out, virtue seemed about to follow, and error and sin reigned triumphant. At length two young men determined to use their influence to check the progress of vice, and looking at the matter philosophically, they went to work. They first formed a debating society; then invited a learned gentleman to give them a series of weekly lectures; established an evening-school, and in these various ways attempted to direct the mind from sinful to innocent amusements. They were successful. The dancing became less frequent, theatrical performances found less encouragement, the circus was denied admittance, and the whole appearance of the town changed, and from being one of the most vicious, it has become one of the most moral and respectable places in the State. A few years wrought an entire change. Had they commenced declaiming against sinful amusements without providing innocent ones, they might have declaimed until the day of doom.

This subject is an important one, and I am glad to see the attention of the public turned to it. Men of thought, and men of action are looking upon it in a philosophical light, and I trust the day is not far distant when young men will not be driven to vicious and degrading amusements to find relaxation.

II. THAT THE VARIOUS AMUSEMENTS WHICH HAVE BEEN DEVISED FOR THE EXPRESS PURPOSE OF GIV-ING RELAXATION HAVE THUS FAR ALL FAILED. The object of amusement is to draw off the mind from more serious and toilsome things, and fit it, after a temporary relaxation, to return to the duties of life with new zeal and ability. Anything which can impair the health, weaken the intellect, corrupt the heart, defeats this object. Anything which brings weariness and exhaustion, and fatigue, and unfits man to perform the duties of life, is not amusement, but vice. Hence, as we look at dancing, at theatrical performances, at gambling, and at the various modes of sinful pleasure, we find that instead of relieving the mind from care, and fitting the body for toil, they are defeating the only object for which relaxation can be sought, they are only adding new cares, new toils, new sorrows. Ask Consumption and she will tell you of the wasting form of the dancer, the hollow cough, and the weary limbs. Go into the chamber of merriment, and you will see men and women dying at half an age. Go to the gambling-saloon, and you will observe the blood-shot eye, the haggard cheek, the trembling lip. Go to the theatre, and you will find the victims of excitement, their minds warped, and their ideas of life all discolored and distorted. Look at any of the schemes of pleasure which have been devised to while away time, to occupy the hours of evening without benefit, and you will find they have failed to accomplish their purpose. They give no relaxation. Perhaps at first, dancing and theatres, were less objectionable than at present, perhaps they gave pleasure and served as recreation; but they have become so corrupted, so debasing, that I see not how a virtuous person can engage in them. The object of their establishment has not been accomplished. And thus it will continue to be with all the vast variety of sinful amusements. However harmless and simple they may be at the beginning, they will grow worse and worse, and instead of serving as pleasant, healthy recreation, will tend to vitiate, corrupt, and impair.

Man was made for usefulness. He was designed by God to get good and do good, and hence any amusement to subserve well its purpose, must be blended with utility. But such is not the case with the throng of sinful pleasures by which we are encompassed. There is no utility about them. They are not formed to benefit, but to amuse; not to instruct, but please. The theatre does not make men wiser, better, or happier. The ball-room does not lighten the load of life, or take one care from the burdened mind. The gaming-table does not make life lighter, or kindle up hope in any desolate soul. If the heart is sad and

bleeding, if the mind is clouded and perplexed, if the
conscience is in trouble, and sorrow is brooding over
the soul, a resort to any of these pleasures will only
add new bitterness to every cup, and gather a denser
darkness around the sinner's path. Thus men will find
it, sooner or later. They may for awhile find what
they call amusement in the vain and sinful inventions
of the age ; they may silence the voice of conscience
for a time, and in the busy whirl of pleasure and
gayety, pass on heedless of the admonitions which are
given them, but the end will come, and these pleasures will prove to be sources of vexation and sorrow

III. SOME AMUSEMENTS, WHICH ARE HARMLESS,
AND WHICH BLEND UTILITY WITH PLEASURE. That
there are such amusements, you are all ready to admit, but the usual objection urged against them is,
that they are tame and un satisfying. With perverted tastes, the followers of the world fail to perceive
the true, substantial pleasure which flows from useful amusements. But with a pure and uncorrupted
taste, with a heart feelingly alive to what is truly
good, useful amusements are full of recreation and
enjoyment. While others fail to give the desired relaxation, these are completely successful ; they unbend the mind awhile from life's severer duties, and
permit it to return to those duties doubly prepared to
perform them. A few of them I will briefly enumerate.

1. *Useful reading.* In these days of book-making, when the press is throwing off its daily and hourly burden of valuable and worthless volumes, we need be at no loss to make a wise and judicious selection to amuse, instruct, and benefit. Books of travel, of history, of science, of philosophy, of morals, of religion, are abundant, and within the reach of all young people. Whatever may be our peculiar feelings and inclinations, tastes and habits, we can find some kind of reading which will benefit us. If we desire to become acquainted with the past, to know how men have lived, and where they were buried, and what have been their habits, volumes of history, written in the various styles of authors having different national and mental peculiarities, and abounding with information of every character, are in our hands. If we have an inclination to travel, and possess not the means for enjoying this privilege, we may find the most delightful accounts of voyages and journeys, and at our own firesides, travel the wide world over. With the author we may ascend the highest mountains, and descend into the lowest caverns; we may visit temples, cathedrals, and pagodas; we may journey to every clime, become familiar with the people of all lands, and ere we have traveled beyond the limits of our own native town, may be acquainted with the customs and manners of all earth's tribes. If we wish to study the sciences, and learn

the discoveries of the wisest men, we have their works, their minds portrayed on paper, spread out before our gaze, and ready for our use. And while we have these, there is no occasion to resort to fiction, tragedy, and dramatic pleasures. The drama has nothing to compare for interest, with the realities of science, and there is nothing in fiction which will equal the realities of history. The drama is tame, and tasteless, compared with the history of the past, and there are scenes every year transpiring on the great theatre of the world, which make even the fictions of the most glowing writers appear insipid. Now reading is a recreation which combines pleasure with utility, amusement with profit. It does not weary the body, it does not exhaust the mind, it does not corrupt the heart. It brings vigor to each, and gives relaxation and change, and fits us for the more laborious and irksome duties of life. An hour spent in the dancing-room brings weariness and sorrow; an hour spent over a useful book, brings pleasure and profit, and expands and enlarges the deathless soul.

2. *Music.* There are some who have little or no desire to cultivate musical talents, but to others, this science is a source of exquisite enjoyment. Indeed were it not for the sweet and melting strains of music, many scenes of mirth and festivity would lose all their charm, the dancing-hall and the theatre would be as dull and senseless as the gambols of a child

Now to the lover of harmony there is no source of recreation more reasonable and delightful. As the laboring man returns from toil, weary and dejected, the sound of music, and the song of his wife or child will cause him to forget his weariness, and lose his dejection. The simple lay will be a balsam for his wounded spirit, and in the midst of sorrow the heart will be glad. Music formed one of the prominent amusements of the ancient Hebrews. They sung everywhere, and mingled melody with joy or sorrow. The royal David with his chief musicians, Asaph, Heman, and Jeduthun, with their four thousand assistants made ceaseless song, and Solomon, his son, the wisest man of his age, had men-singers and women-singers, and Josephus tells us, that the number of musicians employed by him at the dedication of the temple was *two hundred thousand*. The Greeks and Romans had their songs and their instruments of music, and frequently when they went out to battle, it was with the sound of melody. Nor shall we find music under proper circumstances to be wearisome or dissipating. It will give the mind and body relaxation and profit, and fail to impair the intellect or deprave the heart.

> ' Music the fiercest grief can charm,
> And fate's severest rage disarm.
> Music can change pain to case,
> And make despair and madness please ,
> Our joys below it can improve,
> And antedate the bliss above."

There is no science which will assist in the management of children, which will serve to soften down human nature, and make the heart feel, to such an extent, as music. Those therefore who are striving to substitute music for the performances of the stage, and the dissipation of the festive hall, and the midnight revel, deserve the thanks of community; and musical exhibitions, concerts, and performances should be encouraged, not only by the lovers of pleasure, but also by the lovers of morality and religion.

3. *Traveling.* I know that extensive traveling is not within the reach of all, and yet I would recommend it to all who have the pecuniary ability. If a man remains at home all his days, if he shuts himself up within the limits of his own city, and never goes forth to behold the world, and admire the works of God, his soul will be limited and contracted. He will fail to take an enlarged view, and be unable to exert an extensive influence. There is something in an acquaintance with the world, with men and things, which gives the soul breadth and dimension, and fits it to take an ample view of the subjects which are presented. I am aware that traveling is costly; that long journeys involve much expense. All that may be urged on this point will be admitted. But do I not address some young men, who in every five years spend as much in dancing, in theatrical entertainments, and in other dissipating

amusements, as would pay the expense of a visit to Europe, or a voyage to any part of the world. Do I not speak to some, who every year squander enough to defray the expense of a journey through every State in the Union. To those who have the ability, traveling is an entertaining and profitable method of securing relaxation.

4. *Literary lectures.* To afford this kind of relaxation, our lyceums, and lecture courses, have been established. They contribute much to the pleasure and profit of society. They draw together many who would otherwise be in places of depraved and sinful pleasure. These lectures are generally prepared with considerable care, and contain whole volumes condensed. They frequently present subjects which are in themselves dry and uninteresting, and which on the printed page would give but little pleasure to the reader, but the charm of the living speaker is thrown around them, and knowledge is derived which would never be drawn from printed volumes. The value of these lectures is too little known, and too little appreciated. Were they more frequent, and better attended, we should have a more enlightened community, and a more virtuous society. Did they take the place of other degrading and disgusting sources of amusement, we should not so often behold the wrecks of character, and the ruin of unfortunate young men   We should not so often behold the

7

gray hairs of parents brought in sorrow to the grave, or hear them lament so frequently the downfall of their prodigal sons.

5. *Social visiting.* Young men are not fond of visiting. They deem it tedious to call from house to house, to seek an acquaintance with society. But if they would employ more of their time in this manner, they would find it a source of pleasure and profit. They would thus be enabled to make valuable acquaintances, they would see men as they are, and not as they *appear* in public life, they would get a deeper insight into human nature, they would escape the hollow and heartless salutations of public occasions, and be able better to understand "life at home." I am aware that those who congregate in large cities are often destitute of any place which they dare denominate HOME. But others who are more fortunately situated, have a duty devolved upon them by this very fact; a duty, too, which has hardly begun to be understood. In a city like this, the doors of every house should be open to our young people ; they should be invited frequently to visit our families, not as strangers or dependents, but as young men who have no homes and firesides of their own. Let them know that your parlors and your sitting-rooms are always ready to receive them, and when they come give them a cordial welcome.

7. *Social gatherings.* These are somewhat com-

mon in the form of "sewing societies," which young people of both sexes attend. They are connected with the various religious congregations, and are on the whole, productive of good. Though all social gatherings will have some objections attending them, yet they are, at least, innocent substitutes for worse amusements. Every such society should have some benevolent object in view, and in no case should mere enjoyment be substituted for utility. While freedom should be given to all the social feelings, the great fact that we are immortal and accountable, should be made prominent. There are other social gatherings on various occasions, *all* of which I would not recommend. Many of them are turned to vicious purposes, and are calculated to defeat the object for which we seek recreation. There are others in which we may freely engage, in which we may take a part, and by so doing find bodily and mental relaxation. We have been made for society, formed for mutual fellowship, and if we find it not in these harmless, we shall find it in sinful and depraved circles.

> " To view alone,
> The fairest scenes of land and deep,
> With none to listen, and reply
> To thoughts with which my heart beat high,   .
> Were irksome ; for whate'er our mood,
> In sooth, we love not solitude.

8. *Paintings, and other works of art.* To most of us, the paintings of the great masters are in

accessible. Those works which the world has admired are out of our reach; but within a few years
paintings and statuary of less merit have become
abundant. The late works are well-adapted to the
common mind, and though in many cases destitute of
artistic skill, are really valuable in giving us an idea
of the scenery of various countries which we have
never visited. These exhibitions form a pleasant and
profitable mode of securing recreation, and deserve
the patronage of all young people. The artists in almost all cases are young men, and deserve the support of community for the services which they have
rendered. We have the " Voyage to Europe," the
" Scenery of the Rhine ;" the " Views of the Missis-
sippi and Ohio ;" the " Scenery and Battles of Mexico ;" the " Model of Ancient and Modern Jerusa-
lem ;" the " Moving Statuary of the Scriptures,"
and a multitude of others which are all deserving of
notice.

I might mention many other sources of innocent
pleasure, which are combined with utility, but these
will suffice. We are surrounded on all sides with op-
portunities to enjoy ourselves without becoming the
patrons of vice, and if we will, we may secure them.
There is one source of pleasure and relaxation from
toil, which I ought not to omit in this enumera-
tion, a source of pleasure and bliss which exceeds
all others, and is more rational and Godlike, an

avocation in which angels are ceaselessly employed. I refer to

9. *Religion; the public and private worship of God.* I know that to many, the duties of religion would be an intolerable hardship. I am aware that they would find no pleasure in the closet, or in the praying circle, while their hearts remain unchanged, but to others the place of prayer is, of all spots on earth, the best to find calm and holy satisfaction, to obtain relief from sorrow and sin, to unbend the mind from the world's perplexities, and centre it on true and pure objects, and if you will secure that state of mind which will fit you for communion with God, you will find in it a more substantial pleasure, than this poor wretched world affords. It will sweeten every cup which Divine providence puts to mortal lips, and dispel the darkest shadow which ever gathers over the sinner's path.

> "Religion is a glorious treasure,
> The purchase of a Saviour's love;
> It fills the mind with consolation,
> And lifts the soul to things above."

Here I will leave the subject, asking you to give it that attention which its importance demands. As you go out from this house you will find some sinful amusement presenting its claim on every side. As the week rolls away, and you feel the need of recreation and change, a score of objects will present them selves, and hold out their tempting offers.   On every hand you will be beset with vices and seductions.   At such times remember the claims of God and reason Let the fact that you are immortal and accountable, that you are not to perish in the grave, but are to live on after the destruction of matter, and the world's great wreck, and think and act in the vast future, admonish you.   Contemplate yourself as a young man, created by God for a noble purpose, placed in this world as a probationer for the next, to live with angels or with demons forever.   When sin presents its claims, when your associates urge you into paths of vice and folly, and all around are conspiring to shut out the voice of God, and induce thee to destroy and wrong thy nobler nature, do it not.   Thou art immortal, accountable.   Let this thought drive thee back from every path of sin.   God is thy sire, thou art his child !   Let this send thee to his arms.   Remember, that

> " The stars shall fade away, the Sun himself
> Grows dim with age, and Nature sinks in years :
> But thou shalt flourish in immortal youth,
> Unhurt amidst the war of elements,
> The wreck of matter, and the crash of worlds."

It is right that man should be happy ; it is proper for him to seek amusement and enjoyment.   There is nothing in nature, nothing in religion which forbids the full and free enjoyment in a *reasonable* manner.

and to a *reasonable* extent, of all the faculties which God has given us; but while enjoying, we have no right to debase; when seeking pleasure, we have no excuse for plucking the poison-flowers of sin. All within us, and around us, utters impressively, "the way of the transgressor is hard." While the way of life is full of precious tokens of Divine approval, the curse of the Almighty, hangs over the way of death, and though pleasure may be found for a season, and the heart beat gaily in its own fancied, but false security, the end will be as dreadful, as the beginning was fair and deceitful. Every tree in Satan's garden, hangs laden with poisoned fruit, and wo to him who plucks and eats.

LECTURE V.

Do thyself no harm. *Acts*, xvi. 28.

THIS passage of Scripture is a part of one of the most interesting narratives which can be found in any of the sacred writings. It was uttered while Paul was at Philippi, a city of Macedonia. On account of his religious opinions and teachings he had been incarcerated in a dungeon, and in company with Silas had been thrust into the inner prison. With his free spirit, unbroken by the affliction, he praised God at midnight, the whole prison resounded with the melody of a song which had never been heard there before. The prisoners in their cells heard the sweet music. Starting from their slumber, they asked in astonishment, "What is this?" and listened with wrapt attention to the heavenly sound as it echoed on the air of night, and floated in gentle strains through their dark and gloomy dungeons. While they thus sang an earth-

(104)

quake shook the prison, the fetters fell from their chafed limbs, and they rose up, leaving their manacles behind them. Aroused by the noise and confusion of the scene, the jailor arose in terror, and saw the doors of his prison open, and the fetters struck from the limbs of the prisoners, whom he had been charged to keep in safety. Supposing that some had fled, he was alarmed, and in fear lest he should be punished, drew his sword and would have killed himself. Seeing his desperate intention, Paul cried out to him, "Do thyself no harm," and by a declaration that none had escaped, calmed his fears, and induced him to put his sword again into its sheath.

Like the Philippian jailor, men are now doing themselves (in many instances) inconceivable harm. They are their own worst enemies, and are frequently the cause of their own destruction. Thus is it with those who are living in the practice of the sinful amusements of life, and who are bent on the gratification of their carnal desires at the expense of better and holier things. Like a madman they are drawing the sword upon themselves, and doing to their own souls irreparable injury.

Upon the subject of DANGEROUS AMUSEMENTS, I wish this evening to offer a few friendly remarks, and by presenting them to you as they appear to my own mind, induce you to avoid them as destructive to the welfare of this life, and the life to come. In the brief space allowed for a single lecture, I can only glance at a few of the most prominent sources of sinful pleasure, and by the survey of them, lead you to an abhorrence of the whole. I will call your attention then,

To THE DANGEROUS AMUSEMENTS OF OUR TIMES. Their number is legion. They are adapted to high life, and low life, to youth and age, to every condition and rank of human beings. They do not exist alone in crowded cities, and marts of commerce, but make every spot inhabited by man, the scene of their operations. Created by God upright, surrounded with pure and profitable pleasures, man has forsaken them, and sought out many inventions. He has left the pure spring of living water, the fountain which gushes from the hand of God, and hewn out to himself broken cisterns which can hold no water. Fitted for the skies, made by the Creator to look upward, and destined for immortality, man has withdrawn his gaze from Deity, and fixed it on the earth. Dying although he be, he courts disease. Death lurks in his path, clad in the livery of heaven, and he stoops to embrace the monster, and dies. Nothing that he meets in all his progress through life is more deceptive and false, than are the sinful pleasures by which Satan wishes to ensure his destruction. The arch-fiend, who knows well with what material he has to deal, has displayed his infernal wisdom in the devices by which every step of youth is beset. The various amusements of society have been the ruin of thousands, who but for them, might have been upright and respectable. All along the tide of time, are wrecks of characters which have been destroyed by the gilded fascinations of pleasure. And thousands more will be destroyed ere men will open their eyes upon the fearful scenes around them, and arise in all the strength of human nature, to roll back the waves of sorrow. And until this time arrives, these monuments of wrath will stand; like sunken rocks at times concealed from view, they will involve new victims in the snare, and prove the fatal spots where souls are wrecked.

I. *The theatre.* So much has been said of late upon this source of depraved pleasure, that I need not dwell much upon it. All *good* men have united in its condemnation, and all bad men have joined in its support.

> "From first to last it was an evil place,
> And now such scenes are acted there, as made
> The devils blush; and from the neighborhood,
> Angels and holy men, trembling retired."

I do not say that the theatre *cannot* be made a source of innocent amusement; I do not affirm that the drama cannot be made a source of reasonable enjoyment: but I do affirm that it *is* not. Facts which cannot be controverted prove that it has been, and is now, a source of moral corruption. In every city of our great country the theatre has been an aceldama, and many a father has turned his weeping eyes towards it, as the spot where his child was decoyed into sin, and ruined forever. Says Rev. Mr. East, " I called to see a mother ; she was in distress. She not merely wept, but wept aloud. ' O my child !' and she wept again. ' O my child is just committed to prison, and I fear he will never return to his father's house,' and then her tears burst forth, and with all my firmness I could not help weeping with her. I was afraid to ask the cause ; I did not need, for she said, ' O that THEATRE ! He was a virtuous, kind youth, *till that theatre proved his ruin!*' " Nor is this a solitary case. There are mothers throughout New England who are shedding like tears, over like sorrow. It is the opinion of one of the best, most talented, clergymen of our country ; a man of age, observation, and long experience, that more characters are ruined by the theatre, than by any other device of Satan. He says, " I have watched the progress of young men, as they have become the habitual attendants upon the amusements of the stage, and never have I known one to maintain his integrity any length of time." The whole history of theatrical performances, prove that there is about them a corrupting influence, a demoralizing tendency. Exciting and fascinating, they secure a large attendance, and exert a wide influence. The young are dazzled and charmed by the display, and ere they are aware, have ventured too far out upon the sea of indulgence to return. Not many months ago, I visited, at the request of a broken-hearted mother, a young man who was confined in prison. As I entered the cell and introduced myself to him, I saw shame spread over his face, and the blush overcast a countenance from which vice had not as yet removed all trace of beauty. Seating myself by his side, I commenced a kind and cheerful conversation with him. He told me that he had been in that place seven months, and had several more to remain. His heart was bowed with sorrow as he remarked, " that during those seven months, he had heard kind words from only one person — *his mother.*" He described to me the course of crime which had made him an outcast from society. At the age of twenty-two he had a character as fair as ours. His employment was profitable, and he was doing well. But he was induced to attend the theatre. What he saw there pleased him. He went again and again. Soon his income would not support his extravagance. The nightly visit to the play-house must be abandoned, or he must have more money. He endeavored to secure a more lucrative business, but failed. He took upon himself new duties, but the increase of his income was not proportionate to the increase of his expenses. The

gaming-table presented itself, and he became a gambler. From one step to another he advanced in
crime. As his heart grew harder, he became bolder
in sin, and at length committed the crime for which
he was imprisoned. " O," said he to me, with a tone
which I never shall forget, " had I known that I
should have come to this, I would have as soon jump-
ed into the fires of hell, as gone to the theatre."
When I spoke of reformation, he shook his head, and
sighed. " This country is no home for a detected
thief," he said. Upon looking around his room, I
found two books ; a Bible which his mother had given
him, and which had no appearance of having been
read, and the " Wandering Jew," an obscene, disgusting novel. He was a melancholy spectacle of
what the theatre can do, and is doing, to transform
the fair characters of our young people, and change
them from upright members of society to degraded,
detected outcasts. Henry Ward Beecher, in his
strong, truthful language says, speaking of the theatre, " Here are brilliant bars to teach the young to
drink ; here are gay companions to undo in half an
hour, the scruples formed by an education of years ;
here are pimps of pleasure to delude the brain with
bewildering sophisms of license ; here is pleasure, all
flushed in its gayest, boldest, most fascinating forms ;
and few there be who can resist its wiles ; and fewer
yet, who can yield to them, and escape ruin. If you

would pervert the taste, go to the theatre. If you would imbibe false views, go to the theatre. If you would efface as speedily as possible all qualms of conscience, go to the theatre. If you would put yourself irreconcilably against the spirit of virtue and religion, go to the theatre. If you would be infected with each particular vice in the catalogue of depravity, go to the theatre. Let parents, who wish to make their children weary of home and quiet domestic enjoyments, take them to the theatre. If it be desirable for the young to loathe industry and didactic reading, and burn for fiery excitements, and seek them by stealth, or through pilferings if need be, then send them to the theatre."

2. *Dancing.* I am well aware, that there are different grades of vice and depravity connected with this amusement. There are the occasional balls and parties, and the regular weekly, or nightly revel. While of the former we cannot speak in commendation, of the latter we can speak only in terms of entire disapproval. As they are conducted they are sinks of depravity, one of which is sufficient to curse a nation. I am yet to find that there is anything good about them. Contrived for the gratification of the basest passions of the basest classes in society, they become the source of a vast amount of profligacy and debauchery. They neither tend to give relaxation to the exhausted body, nor the care-worn mind;

they do not implant in the soul one single virtuous sentiment; they do not strengthen in any mind the virtuous teachings of home, but everywhere are found to be prolific causes of corruption and death. Could all those who are ruined every year in large cities, by this vicious amusement, be brought together, what a spectacle would be presented. Men who are now apologizing for the vice, would stand aghast; parents who are sending their children to these sinks of corruption would as soon send them into a nest of vipers; young men who are bartering their souls away for the miserable mirth, would fly from it, as from the door of hell. The broken-down tradesman, the ruined mechanic, the once studious lawyer, would appear before us, limping from the midnight carousal, to bear witness to the damning influence of this school of infamy. Once respected, once prosperous in life, once beating with high hopes; now tossed by passion, and driven by the storms of vice. Females would come, daughters and sisters, who awhile since, suspicion dare not touch, and on whose cheek the blush of shame had never been seen, now wearing vice like a garment, every feature distorted, every sign of innocence blotted out, every trace of virtue gone. This is no tale of fancy. You have only to look around you to have it painfully confirmed. I knew a family awhile since who were living in the enjoyment of many of life's blessings. The husband and the wife were young, and when I saw them first, a lovely child was twining its arms around the mother's form. A year rolled away, and there was a change. God in his awful providence had removed the child, and left the parents in sorrow. Home now seemed dreary, and instead of seeking solace in the Saviour, they fled to the dance and the revel. Soon the woe commenced. The mother threw aside her mourning for the gay attire of the ball-room, and each of them began to drink the bitter waters of vice. Affection for each other fled; strife took the place of contentment and quiet; a separation ensued; the husband fled, and the wife, young, interesting and intelligent, has entered upon a course of crime which will end in complete ruin. A happy family has been destroyed, the hearts of friends have been distressed, and the vows of marriage recklessly trampled under foot.

3. *Gambling.* This sort of amusement is generally regarded as a crime. Those who uphold the theatre and the dance, make no plea for this. The law looks upon it as a doubtful employment, and none but those engaged in it, are willing to be its defenders. And yet there are few sources of corruption more fascinating and deceptive. All men want money, and when the prospect of securing a large sum in a single night, is held up before us, the eyes are dazzled and blinded. Compared with a game of chance, the slow process of making a fortune over an

8

anvil or plough, appears to the young exceedingly difficult, and they are often led to the gaming-table, in order to become rich sooner. Then there is something in gaming, when considered as an amusement merely, which is well-calculated to captivate. The uncertainty, the excitement, the all-absorbing interest, lead the mind astray, and he who becomes addicted to the vice, and learns to love it, will find himself bound in chains stronger than iron. Within the last few years gaming has become exceedingly prevalent; children are gambling in the streets, their sires are gambling in low cellars, while our fashionable young men are pursuing the same employment in gay and gilded saloons. In almost every street your ears are saluted by the sound of the rolling ball, and the clattering dice, and the melancholy evidence of the prevalence of this vice is on every side. And the result will be a community of dishonest men; a vicious, depraved society.

The idea that a man can be honest while he is a confirmed gambler, is absurd. Gambling saps the principle of honesty, and makes a man a villain in a night. The record of this vice is full of cases which are fearfully illustrative of the truth of this position. In a short time a man will learn to cheat his victim without mercy. He will lead him to the bar, and induce him to drink, and when his brain is on fire will lead him back to the board.

and rob him of his all. He may know that he has a starving wife and child at home, but he cares not for that. He may know that the safety of the man's reason, and *life*, and SOUL, may depend on the game, but he cares not. He will cheat him, even if he knows his wife and child will starve, or die broken-hearted; he will play and rifle his pockets, though he may believe all the while, that the poor wretch will be driven to madness, to suicide, to hell. The tender mercy of the confirmed gambler is cruel. Gold is his god, and to secure it, he would barter away the souls of his own children. I know of no vice which so effectively hardens the heart, destroys all tender feeling, and deadens the soul to things which are excellent, as does gambling. The theatre and the dance, destructive as they are, are not to be compared with it in this respect. Dr. Nott says, "The finished gambler has no heart; he would play at his brother's funeral, he would gamble upon his mother's coffin." A fact is related on good authority,* of gamblers who wished to show their utter contempt for all sacred things, and their entire disregard of all that men deem sacred and divine. After various deeds of folly and madness, which exhibited their recklessness, they entered at night the charnel-house of a cathedral, and took from its resting-place a corpse which had been buried the same day. Up

* Rev. W. B. Tappan.

through the narrow passage, they bore the person of
the dead, uttering low jokes and blasphemous expressions. With their clay-cold load they arrived in the
cathedral, passed within the chancel, lighted up one
of the candles of the altar, and then placing the
corpse in a chair by the communion-table, gathered
around it and engaged in a game of chance.

4. *Social drinking.* Intemperance is insidious. It
does not come at once with its burning streams to
consume the heart of its victim, but slowly and
gradually drags itself along, taking one fortress after another, until the fashionable, genteel, moderate
drinker has become the reeling, bloated, degraded
drunkard.   There is something in the idea of taking
a social glass with a friend, or drinking a cup of
sparkling wine on some public occasion, exceedingly
pleasant. The young fail to perceive the danger of
the practice. They cannot see how it is, that a
man is led on from moderation to brutal excess, and
hence use the wine-cup freely, and without fear of any
evil consequences. The idea that he shall become a
drunkard, does not enter into the mind of the young
man when he sips the poison. And thus it has evei
been with those who have become intemperate. Not
one of all the thousands who have gone down to a
drunkard's grave, and have entered upon the scenes
of a drunkard's eternity, ever supposed that he should
be a beastly, degraded inebriate. Such an end never

presented itself to the mind of any young man, as for the first time he drank his social glass. But step by step, the habit grew upon him; day by day the fatal spell was thrown around him; deeper and deeper he descended into the vortex of wretchedness, until the last lamp which shed its light upon his path was put out, the last star of hope sank in darkness.

I am perhaps addressing those who occasionally make use of intoxicating drinks, and who on social occasions deem it well to take the cup of wine without hesitation. You do not perceive any signs of danger, and should one remonstrate with you personally, you would consider it an insult. "Can I not govern myself?" you would ask with outraged feelings. "Can I not drink when I please, and let it alone when I please?" "Have I no power over my appetite and passions?" The same questions others have asked, and yet been hurried into the whirlpool of drunkenness. Others, when remonstrated with, have been as indignant as yourself, but have ultimately found that the cup was poison, that death lurked beneath its brim, that the deathless worm was coiled up there, that it burned the soul with deathless flame. I have read somewhere of a man who kept a tiger in his house. He had secured the animal when it was quite young, and by kindness and gentleness had apparently subdued its ferocious and bloodthirsty disposition. So attached to his pet did he become, that he took the creature to bed with him at night, and let it follow him in his travels. Friends remonstrated, and urged the nature of the animal, and predicted danger. The foolish man laughed at their fears, and ridiculed the idea of danger. At length he went to sleep at night as usual with the beast by his side. Turning in his bed he drew his hand across one of the paws of his favorite. The wound streamed with blood. The tiger tasted it. His ferocious nature which had been curbed for years was aroused, and when the morning came, all that remained of his master was a bleeding, mangled corpse. The man who sports with intemperance in any form, who drinks moderately or immoderately is tampering with the tiger. He will realize the truth of Scripture, " at last it biteth like a serpent, and stingeth like an adder."

5. There are other sources of sinful and dangerous amusement, which I need not mention. If you turn your gaze over the surface of society, you will find abundant evidence upon this subject. Everywhere will meet your eye the crowds of men and women seeking pleasure in paths that lead to death, and on every hand will appear the wrecks of character which strew the tide of time. A few objections to all sinful pleasures, will close this discourse.

1. *They abuse time.* Time was given us for a high purpose. It was designed as a season of probation. In it, man is to fit himself for eternity, and

prepare his soul for a crown in heaven. He has no right to squander it in any of the vain employ-ments which I have this evening enumerated. We are accountable to God, and of nothing will he require a more strict account than of our time. If that is wasted and abused, his most severe judgments will fall upon the guilty head. And what waste of time can be more shameful than that of the dancer, or the stage-player? It is a sad and fearful sight to behold a being created for immortality, having a deathless soul, and soon to stand before God, leaving the purpose for which his Maker has designed him, and spending the time which will soon run out, in capering around a violin until midnight, or watching the grimaces of some ridiculously dressed actor, as he attempts to mimic the poor forlorn objects of human woe. If there is one scene on earth, which is empty, vain, and trifling, it is that which the dancing-hall exhibits. The gambler hopes to gain gold, but dancers can hope for nothing but exhaustion, weariness, and disease. Dressed in gilt and tinsel, looking more like some specimens of the brute creation than human beings, they whirl and tumble about like idiots, or shakers. One grand jumble will not satisfy them, but hour after hour must be spent in the unhealthy, unreasonable, unmeaning service. And how will such give an ac-count of their time to God? Has he given them the precious boon of life for such a purpose? Has he made man immortal that he might spend thus, his existence upon the earth? Not at all! God had no such design in view, and he must look down upon these sources of depraved pleasure with infinite abhorrence. If the waste of time was the only objection which could be urged against them, it would be enough. It would be sufficient to brand them with divine and human disapprobation. It would be enough to induce every son and daughter of Adam to abjure them as destructive to the best interests of the human family.

2. *They are destructive to health.* This you all know. The man must be insane who denies that drinking and dancing are calculated to sap the energies of the system and destroy life. Were half the vigorous constitutions destroyed by an attendance upon the house of God, that are ruined by the amuse ments which are spread around us in such profusion, the voice of the whole community would demand that houses of public worship should be abolished. Many individuals are horror struck, if a protracted meeting is held, or, if on the evenings of the week, meetings are prolonged an half hour beyond the usual length. And yet the persons who make such an outcry see no objection to dancing meetings if they are continued until morning. They are afraid that Christians will suffer, if they sit a single hour in the praying circle, even though they be arrayed in warm,

comfortable clothing, and yet will resort to the dancing hall in the most unbecoming and uncomfortable
apparel, and deem it no outrage upon the laws of
nature. When this matter shall be seen in its proper
light, it will be found that to the sinful amusements,
the sexton is to a great extent indebted for his trade ;
that more lives are lost by them, than by war. There
should (if justice had its rule), be a hospital beside
every dancing hall, and every tippling shop in our
land, and the broken down specimens of humanity
who keep these laboratories of death, should behold
the destruction which they cause.

3. *They lead to extravagance and prodigality.*
The road is not a long one, from affluence to poverty,
when vice has become a source of amusement and
daily recreation. We have not to travel far to
find sad and solemn lessons, teaching the influence
of vicious pleasure upon the purse and pocket.
Every city has them. They throng the temple of
memory. They are living all around us. The great
cause why so many young men are obliged to aban-
don business, and retire from the scenes of youth, is,
not because commercial embarrassments have spread
over the land, not because business is not profitable,
but because vicious pleasure is unprofitable, because
a course of vice will swallow up the most lavish income, because the ceaseless cry of these depraved
pleasures is like that of the daughter of the leech,

Give, give. To a young man accustomed to find enjoyment in the vicious amusements of the day, there is no end to expenses. They come thicker and faster, like the snow flakes of winter. They multiply and increase every day, and soon the course of folly must be broken up, or the means for continuing these excesses, furnished from some other quarter. Do you ask the cause of so much bankruptcy? Look for a reply to the sinful amusements of our large cities, pursued by their ten thousand votaries. Do you ask the cause of so much moral delinquency? of so much dishonesty? so much forgery, and theft, and wrong? Go, for an answer, to the sin-stained pleasures of the young. Do you ask the cause of extravagance, prodigality, and suffering? Go to the lighted hall, the playhouse, and the gay saloon, and you have the reply.

> "Vice drains our cellar dry,
> And keeps our larder clean; puts out our fires,
> And introduces hunger, frost, and woe,
> Where peace and hospitality might reign."

4. *They are unnatural.* Man does not need them. They are perversions of our nature, and produce misery only. They do not bring relaxation and relief, but sorrow and distress. They are wholly unnecessary. God has given us pure pleasures in abundance. He has surrounded us with an endless variety of charms, and made us to enjoy them. The angels might as well descend to earth in the vain hope

of finding more bliss here, than beside the shining
throne, as man leave the pure joys and pleasures
which God has given, to grasp those which Satan has
devised for his destruction. Says an eloquent writer,
" Upon this broad earth, perfumed with flowers, scent-
ed with odors, brilliant in colors, vocal with echo-
ing and re-echoing melody, I take my stand against
all demoralizing pleasure. Is it not enough that our
Father's house is so full of dear delights, that we must
wander prodigal to the swineherd for husks, and to
the slough for drink ? When the trees of God's heri-
tage bend over our heads, and solicit our hand to
pluck the golden fruitage, must we still go in search
of the apples of Sodom — outside fair, and inside
ashes ? Men will crowd the circus to hear clowns,
and see rare feats of horsemanship ; but a bird may
poise beneath the very sun, or flying downward swoop
from the high heavens ; then flit with graceful ease,
hither and thither, pouring liquid song as if it were a
perennial fountain of sound, no man cares for that.
Upon the stage of life, the vastest tragedies are performing in every act ; nations pitching headlong to
their final catastrophe ; others, raising their youthful
forms to begin the drama of their existence. The
world of society is as full of exciting interest, as nature is full of beauty. The great dramatic throng of
life is hustling along, the wise, the fool, the clown,
the miser, the bereaved, the broken-hearted. Life

mingles before us smiles and tears, sighs and laugh-
ter, joy and gloom, as the spring mingles the winter
storm and summer sunshine. To this vast theatre
which God hath builded, where stranger plays are
seen than ever authors writ, man seldom cares to
come. When God dramatizes, when nations act,
or all human kind conspire to educe the vast catastrophe, men sleep and snore ; and let the busy scene
go on, unlooked, unthought upon, and turn from all
its varied magnificence to hunt out some candle-
lighted hole, and gaze at drunken ranters, or cry at
the piteous virtue of harlots in distress."

5. *They are heart-corrupting, and soul-destroying.*
Were the effects of vicious amusements confined to
this life, were the waste of time, the abuse of health,
the extravagance and prodigality, all the evil which
could flow from them, they might be sought with less
guilt than at present. But they have immediate influence upon the soul of man, and are doubtless the
cause of the destruction of thousands. The day of
judgment will alone reveal the influence of depraved
pleasures in peopling that world where no light is,
and where the wail of sorrow is ever heard. They
contribute essentially to deaden the heart to holy influences, to scar the conscience, and prepare the victim to go out into blackness and darkness. Those
who are accustomed to find pleasure in such scenes,
are well aware, that they are inconsistent with reli-

gion, and the contemplation of heavenly objects; that they turn the mind away from God, and blind the eyes to all the dangers of the future.

It is a sad sight, to see men so nobly made, with such a lofty destiny before them, with so many high hopes of future good, pursuing the miserable phantoms of this life, and choosing pleasure and sinful mirth, while heaven and immortality should be the objects of their choice. And I presume they will continue in this course of madness until death calls them away to the retributions of eternity. As it was in the days of Noah, so shall it be in the coming of the Son of man. Men will eat and drink, work and play, be sorrowful and merry until the end come, and the wicked shall be destroyed. And I fear that some will be so attached to their pleasures that they will continue to sport with judgment, until the power of vengeance shall burst upon them.

I know not as I can better close this discourse, than by relating an incident which is said to have occurred while the French army occupied the city of Moscow. Of its truth or falsity, I have no means of knowing. A party of officers and soldiers determined to have a military levee, and for this purpose chose the deserted palace of a Russian nobleman, in the vault of which a large quantity of powder had been deposited. That night the city was set on fire. As the sun went down, they began to assemble. The females who followed the fortunes of the French forces, were decorated for the occasion. The gayest and noblest of the army were there, and merriment reigned over the crowd. During the dance the fire rapidly approached them; they saw it coming, but felt no fear. At length the building next to the one which they occupied was on fire. Coming to the windows, they gazed upon the billows of fire which swept upon their fortress, and then returned to their amusement. Again and again they left their pleasure, to watch the progress of the flames. At length the dance ceased, and the necessity of leaving the scene of merriment became apparent to all. They were enveloped in a flood of fire, and gazed on with deep and awful solemnity. At length the fire communicating to their own building, caused them to prepare for flight, when a brave young officer, named Carnot, waved his jeweled glove above his head, and exclaimed, " One dance more, and defiance to the flame." All caught the enthusiasm of the moment, and, " One dance more, and defiance to the flame," burst from the lips of all. The dance commenced, louder and louder grew the sound of music, and faster and faster fell the pattering footsteps of dancing men and women, when suddenly they heard a cry, " The fire has reached the magazine, fly! fly! for life!" One moment they stood, transfixed with horror; they did not know the magazine was there, and ere they re covered from their stupor, the vault exploded, the building was shattered to pieces, and the dancers were hurled into a fearful eternity.

Thus will it be in the final day. Men will be as careless as were those ill-fated revellers. Methinks the hour has come, and I stand upon an eminence from which I behold the vices and amusements of earth. I warn them, and tell them, that in such an hour as they think not, the son of man cometh. With jeering laugh, they ask, " Where is the promise of his coming ?" I bid them prepare to meet their God. They reply, " Pleasure is our God." I tell them of an awful judgment ; a miserable eternity ; and crying " priestcraft," they again engage in the noisy revel. Soon an awful rumbling is heard in the heavens. A thousand voices tell them, that the angels are rolling out the judgment throne. They reply, " One dance more, and defiance to that throne." Suddenly the stars go out, the moon turns to blood, all nature is convulsed, and universal panic seizes the hearts of all men, when, horror struck, I see some Carnot, turn his bloodshot eyes upon the burning world, and waving his jeweled hand above his head, exclaim, " One dance more, and defiance to that flame," and ere that dance is done, the bolt is sped, the magazine of the universe explodes, and *the time to dance is gone.* GONE FOREVER, FOREVER.

LECTURE VI.

For riches are not forever; and doth the crown endure to every generation? *Proverbs*, xxvii. 24.

EW men have had a clearer view of the entire emptiness of all worldly good, than the writer of the book of Proverbs. He had measured the world in which he lived, and gauged its depths of happiness. He had ascended the highest pinnacle of human observation, and gazed upon all the pursuits and pleasures of mankind. He had wandered up and down the world, and found in the cottage and the palace, the same unsatisfying and unsubstantial bliss. He had secured riches, honor, friends, and pleasure, but amid them all, he could not forget that he was mortal. Like a wise man, he endeavored to profit by what he learned, and instead of placing his whole dependence on fleeting and transitory possessions, sought by divine aid, the riches of incorruptible and imperishable worth.

(128)

The results of his meditations, he has given us in the book which has been so appropriately designated, "The Book of Proverbs." In that book is gathered the full experience of a man who had an intimate acquaintance with human life, and who from the cradle to the grave had studied it; an experience given in a form, at once calculated to attract the attention and benefit the reader; a book of sentences and sentiments, the whole of which constitutes one of the most beautiful systems of moral ethics, which was ever placed in the hands of a young man. The extract from that book which I have read as my text, will be the basis of a lecture this evening upon WEALTH AND FAME.

I would not, of course, be understood to condemn the acquisition of wealth, or the pursuit of fame, altogether. I would not wish to check one laudable desire for the things of life, or quench a single aspiration of the mind for the applause of others. There is nothing wrong in the accumulation of property; there is nothing wrong in a desire to have our deeds approved by our fellow-men. Some of the best and purest men of the world have been men of vast fortunes and unbounded fame, and that man who despises either of them, exhibits his folly. The only caution which the Bible gives, is, that we use them well, and not be inordinately attached to them. It sanctions the pursuit of riches to a proper degree,

9

and informs us that the *love* of money, and not money itself, is the root of all evil. Placed as we are in this world, it is our *duty* to secure property, if we can by honest and laudable means. God has made our comfort and convenience in this life somewhat dependent on riches. He has surrounded us with wants and wishes which money alone can gratify, and in a hundred ways pointed out to us the propriety of laboring for the useful and necessary means of subsistence. A proper and praiseworthy desire to have a competency is not a sin. It has nothing in it of a miserly character, and has been encouraged and allowed by God in all ages of the world. Those young men, therefore, who are honestly laboring to amass wealth, in hope that it will make them more useful in life, and help them better to benefit man, and glorify God, are doing right, and deserve the encouragement of the wise and good. They only are to be condemned, who are striving to grow rich by dishonest means, or, who after having secured property, use it for their own selfish gratification. I may be mistaken, but I think God looks from heaven with pleasure upon the busy crowds of human life, who are diligent in business, and amassing property that they may spend it in his service. I am well aware that gold has a tendency to corrupt the heart, and as a general thing, a man's soul becomes frozen and deathlike to just the extent of his riches; but this arises wholly from the fact that money is perverted from its legitimate use, that it is made the occasion of sin, that it is loved more than the Being who gave it. You will there fore remember, as I pass through this lecture, that I condemn only an inordinate desire for riches.

The same remarks may be made of *fame.* Fame is defined to be a favorable report of one's character; praise given to a man because of his real or supposed good deeds. Certainly nothing can be wrong in a desire for this. God has created us with a disposition to please our fellow men, and receive their approval. And this we find to be one of the ties which bind society together. But for this, man would act without regard to the feelings of his neighbors, and human life would become one wild scene of contention and confusion. The desire to be respected by our fellow men, is a proper desire. It restrains from vice hundreds, who but for this, would rush into sin. It leads to self-respect, and is one of the pillars of human character. Strike it down, and you remove one of the strong inducements to virtue, and leave the young without a motive which now operates in behalf of morality with tremendous force. Instead therefore of checking the desire to please others, it should be encouraged. The young should be taught that self-respect, and the respect of community, are both essential to success in life, and early led by honesty, rectitude, and piety, to gain the confidence and esteem of society. But fame is not always pursued for this purpose alone. Like money, it has its worshippers who are determined to secure it, at the hazard of all the other blessings of this life, and the richer blessings of the life to come. With many, fame has changed into a frightful ambition, absorbing all the more lovely and amiable traits of character, and changing man into a blinded, deluded admirer of a fantom which will disappear in an hour.

Thus money and fame, instead of being the blessings which God designed, become sources of iniquity, upon which He must look with peculiar disapprobation and displeasure. You will allow me therefore to offer a few remarks at this time, upon *the folly of an inordinate attachment to wealth and fame.*

1. *They are fluctuating and uncertain.* All who have observed the progress of the world's great changes, must have felt the fearful uncertainty of earthly honors and emoluments. Though all past history has had its changes, and the record of every nation is full of tokens of falling greatness, yet to our times has been left the task of proving most conclusively to the charmed and cheated world, that all earthly honor, and ambition, and riches, are as fluctuating and unstable as the tossed waves of the foaming sea. The last half century has been full of changes, in both private and public life. Single fortunes, and the fortunes of nations, have been gained

and lost Private individuals and public men have risen to stations of honor and opulence, and fallen as suddenly. The world has been dazzled by meteors, which have flashed athwart the sky, and disappeared, leaving the world in darkness. Perhaps there never has been a time of such political and commercial embarrassment and change. The whole world seems to be resting on the hollow bosom of a volcano. Stability is found nowhere. The church and the state are heaving with internal disorders. Life is convulsed, and the shaking pillars of human society attest the precarious character of all earthly ambition. Similar changes to those which are occurring in great states and nations, are found in every department of life, though on a smaller scale. From the tradesman who acts upon his narrow capital of a few hundred dollars, up through all the ranks of wealth to the man who sports and jests with thousands, and is in earnest only when he deals with millions, there is commotion. From the little province, which has scarcely found a place upon the map, and whose insignificance has denied it a record on the pages of history, up to the great kingdoms whose thrones turn upon the world's centre, and whose political economy is interwoven with the very texture of civilized life, there have been agitating and distressing changes.

Men who a few years ago, were rich and increased in goods, having need of nothing, are now bankrupt;

their fortunes are scattered to the winds of heaven, their rich estates are occupied by others, their proud mansions are inhabited by those who awhile since lived in poverty, and all the tokens of their former wealth are gone. Men who not long ago, heard their names chanted by an admiring crowd of human beings, now hear them pronounced with scorn and derision. Sovereigns who imagined themselves seated securely on their thrones, have been driven into vagabondage, and now are eating the bread of disgrace and poverty. Kings have become slaves, and slaves are changed to kings. The wheel of fortune is turning every hour, and those who are in affluence to-day, know not where they will be to-morrow. To illustrate the point more clearly, I will refer to a few changes which have occurred in France, a nation which at the present time is drawing considerable attention, a nation which has seen as many fearful revolutions as perhaps any other on the globe, and been as often deluged in blood and crime.

A little more than fifty years ago, Louis XVI. was seated firmly upon the throne of that ill-fated kingdom. His reign was a weak, but splendid one. He had assumed the reins of government under favorable auspices, and for awhile was the idol of the people. His court was the centre of beauty, fashion, and splendor, and he rode upon the full tide of popular applause. If we could have looked upon

the monarch then, we should have regarded his case
as one of the best specimens of permanent power.
He seemed so strongly entrenched in the affections
of the people, so honored by the esteem of other nations, so surrounded by servile armies, so favored by
the god of wealth, that none would have predicted his
sad end. But the wave of popularity which attended
him in the early part of his administration, and bore
him on to fortune, was deceitful. The voice which
shouted his name with rapture, was calling for his
blood. Honored as he was, wealthy as he had been,
he found but a single step from the monarch's throne
to the block of the malefactor; but one step from the
emoluments of office, and the kingly prerogatives, to
the death of ignominy. The heaving storm of revolution fell not on him alone. His beautiful, accomplished, and high-born queen, Marie-Antoinette, followed him to the scaffold. Bound on a cart, sitting
on the coffin which she was soon to fill with her cold
corpse, she rode along, the widow of a beheaded king,
to her own execution. Crowds of men and women,
who had followed her with admiration not long before,
lined the streets through which she passed, but offered
no assistance, and uttered no sympathy; and when
her trunkless head was elevated on a pike before
their eyes, they shouted, "The tyrants have fallen."
Scarcely had this wild scene passed away, ere Napoleon Bonaparte emerged from his obscurity, and by

extraordinary energy lifted himself into the affections of the people, and the offices of trust. From one step to another, he ascended, until the imperial crown was placed by his own hands upon his head. Each succeeding month clustered new glory around his administration, and he soon became the master of Europe, the wonder of the world. He made kings, and deposed them. He sported with thrones and states, as a child with the leaves of a broken flower. He had wealth, fame, glory, success, all of them. But alas! earthly greatness is precarious. In one day, the glory of his arms became dim, the lustre of his crown faded, the sceptre fell from his palsied hand, and he fled, an exile and a wanderer to a distant home. How strikingly does his short, eventful life, exhibit the vanity of human ambition. A monarch yesterday; to-day a slave. Yesterday, flushed with conquest, a continent fleeing before him; to-day pining in solitude, and perhaps poisoned by the government into whose hand he had given himself for protection.

Then followed Louis Philippe, the *golden* monarch. He deemed wealth and fame substantial, when founded on standing armies, and on the ignorance of the people. Hence, he suppressed all revolutionary publications, enlarged his standing army, procured a bullet-proof coach, doubled his guard, and made his power appear invincible and his throne impregnable.

But in an hour the tide of change swept them all away. The throne was torn from its place, and burned in the streets of Paris, the sceptre was broken to pieces by an infuriated mob, the signs of royalty were scattered before the wild commotion, and the king and his family fled into exile, without money enough in his purse to purchase a change of garment.

Other nations of the earth, though not so prominent as the one to which I have referred, are all undergoing, more or less, really the same process. Scarcely a throne in Europe is secure, and fame and wealth are found to be as uncertain as the whistling wind. Even ecclesiastical fame, and the revenue which is drawn from extensive church organizations are not sure. We see a potentate, who has claimed to be the "Vicegerent of God," driven from the episcopal palace, and seeking a home in a dishonored and unknown spot.

Nor in our own country, is wealth and fame more certain. Some who live and move among us, clad in rags and poverty, were born heirs of extensive possessions, but those possessions have wasted away. As a general thing a fortune runs itself out, ere it reaches the fourth generation, and often a single lifetime is sufficient to change the pecuniary circumstances of a multitude of men. A single failure will sometimes involve a hundred firms in ruin, and lead down a hundred families to abject poverty. A single conflagration which sweeps along the crowded streets of a city, consuming property, will often destroy the hard earnings of many years, and leave toiling men to die in sorrow, destitute of enough to purchase a winding-sheet. Human life is one constant scene of migration from affluence to poverty, a shifting panorama of good and evil.

Nor does *fame* in republics, have anything more of stability, than wealth. Each year presents us with new candidates for popular applause, and consigns the favorites of previous years to oblivion. Our political ingratitude is a marked feature of our national history. Men who have toiled long and well, are denounced for some difference in political opinion, and their places in the government and in halls of legislation, filled with those who have no claim to popular favor. And thus it will continue to be, while the human mind remains the same as at present, and he who is dependent upon the mad shout of the populace, which is as unstable as water, will soon find that his station is one of precarious and doubtful character. In the times of Christ, our divine Saviour, he was made the object of ridicule at one time, and of praise at another time. His reputation was tossed upon the wave of inconstant human passion, and his name shouted at one period with rapture, and at another period with derision. He lived, the sport of changing man ; he died, the victim of popular indignation.

He heard the shout, "Hosanna, hosanna, to the Son of David;" and the cry, "Crucify him, crucify him," sounded in his ears, as it was echoed out by the same multitude.

Such being the precarious character of wealth and fame, I would suggest that they be not made the chief objects of pursuit. There is a purer wealth, there is a more exalted honor, which cometh down from heaven. While I would urge a proper interest in the acquisition of property and a good character, I would suggest that wealth and honor are needed in the world to come, and if *these* be ours, the failure to secure temporal wealth and applause will be of but little consequence.

· 2. *They fail to secure permanent happiness.* Long ago it was proved that things external cannot secure permanent peace and pleasure.

"The conscious mind is its own awful world,"

and if this is in commotion, no external circumstances can give it rest. Hence we have found some of our most wealthy men to be the most miserable of all. Surrounded by all the charms of luxury and splendor, having every wish gratified, and every desire fulfilled, they walk on earth the moving monuments of woe. The notion is a false one, that happiness depends upon wealth. It is not true, that our most wealthy men are the most happy. Facts are against it. Riches

must be attended with care and sorrow, and generally, the more wealth a man has, the fewer will be
his hours of pleasure. I doubt whether the man who
has thousands at command, who is enabled to look
abroad upon extensive fields, and watch for returning
vessels, is as happy as the day laborer, who owns
not the roof which covers him, and who knows not
how long he shall have food for his children. The
one, has riches and crushing cares; the other, has
penury and peace. The one trusts in his laden ship,
in the income of his stocks, in the safety of his invest-
ments; the other, trusts the God who heareth the
young ravens when they cry, and looks for food and
raiment to the

> " Glorious Giver, who doeth all things well."

Nor will *fame* secure peace of mind, and give rest to
the troubled conscience. Men have tried it, and
failed. They have secured the breath of popular applause, they have heard their names mingled with
sweet strains of music, but found the heart within,
restless and unsatisfied. The highest pinnacle of
earthly ambition has been attained, but the " aching
void" has not been filled, nor can it be. As well
might we attempt to satisfy the desire for food with
husks and thorns, as to satisfy the longings of immortality with the transient and unmeaning praises of an
excited crowd. It is said of Alexander, that when

he had secured the world's homage, and covered the earth with the fame of his conquests, he sat down and wept, because there were no more kingdoms and states to conquer. He had wealth, fame, glory; but they did not give him happiness. Had he found another world and made himself master of it, he would have been no nearer the point at which he aimed. Other men whose fame has been world-wide, have given unequivocal evidence, that they had no enjoyment in the things around them, and fame and riches instead of being sources of pleasure, have proved to be sources of sorrow and distress. We are sadly deceived in respect to these things. There is a glitter, a splendor, around the rich man's gold; there is a charm to applause and honor, which cheats the blinded throng. The headache and the heart-ache, cometh alike to rich and poor, noble and ignoble. All the gold which can be found in yonder newly dis-covered mines, cannot drive away the sorrow which unbidden and uncalled, will rush into the temple of the soul. The loudest blast of Fame's burnished trumpet, cannot make melody to a heart oppressed with sorrow, and bowed with guilt. Go ask the Astors, Brookses, Lawrences, and others, who have accumulated large fortunes, and they will tell you, that the mere possession of wealth, is not the promi-nent source of pleasure, that they were as happy when they were poor men, as when their fortunes had increased to millions. Go ask the proudest military chieftain that ever drew a sword, or put a trumpet to his lips; go ask the man most famed for wisdom, skill, and eloquence, and they will both tell you, that fame is an empty blast, and has no power to satisfy the cravings of a deathless soul. Gather in one spacious apartment all the wealthy ones, and the honored of the earth, and you will find no class of men in the wide world who bear so many marks of care, and wear so many traces of sorrow, as do these favored sons of Adam.

> "It is the mind that makes the body rich;
> And as the sun breaks through the darkest clouds,
> So honor peereth in the meanest habit;
> What! is the jay more precious than the lark,
> Because his feathers are more beautiful?
> And is the adder better than the eel,
> Because his painted skin contents the eye."

Certainly not! Nor is the man of wealth and fame, more truly great, and wise, and happy, because he is more favored than his fellows. Wealth and fame, are often like the feathers of the jay, and the skin of the adder, given irrespective of a man's virtues or vices. The pleasant plumage, does not make the jay sing more sweetly; the painted skin, does not detract from the poisonous nature of the adder. The adder is the adder still, with all his beauty; and the rich man with all his wealth and honor, remains a poor sorrow-stricken child of earth. Tell me, ye youthful aspirants for gold and silver, ye who are disposed to leave home and friends, and all the endearments of civilized life, tell me, what a fortune is worth, which cannot purchase exemption from a single pain of body, a single sorrow of the heart? Tell me, what the plaudits of the world are worth which cannot ease the guilty conscience, or wipe away one stain of guilt?

3. *Unreasonably loved, they lead to crime.* I have shown that wealth may be acquired, and fame pursued, to a certain extent. Well would it be for man, if he would stop where God has set the bounds, but in many cases he will not. The mind which is bent on fame, will pursue it at the hazard of all that is truly good. This we have seen in all past history. Principle has been sacrificed, true nobility of soul trodden under foot, the rights of man disregarded, the interests of the undying soul placed in jeopardy, that some ambitious tyrant might have his name recorded

> "Among the few immortal ones,
> That were not born to die."

Wealth has been sought at the same sacrifice, and many to gain it, have lost all that is really valuable. Well does the word of God declare, that "The love of money is the root of all evil." It makes the robber, the gambler, the murderer. It leads to all kinds of crime and degradation. A "haste to be rich," has filled the world with dishonesty and fraud, and plunged many into eternity, covered with the foulest crimes. Hence, our desires on this point cannot be too carefully controlled. An inordinate desire to se- cure the applause of the world, will lead to an aban- donment of the great principles of right and integrity. Under the present constitution of things, a man can- not be universally popular, without lowering the stan dard of his character. A *truly* good man, the people are not yet prepared to love. Popular opinion is di- vided, and the "baser sort" will not honor a man who stands up against their crimes, in the dignity of a pure character. Hence, we find that all good men have their enemies, all virtuous men their opposers. Christ, our great example, was called "Beelzebub," and harsher terms have been applied to the members of his household. Consequently the great temptation to young men is, to relinquish their independence of character, bow to the discordant elements which are around them, and purchase at such a price, the favor of the world. This is especially the case with politi- cal men. Communities change so frequently, that our public men are kept turning continually, until we scarcely know where to find a man, who has become deeply entangled in the intricacies of party politics.

In like manner, an absorbing desire for gold, will lead to fatal results. He who is determined to be rich at any sacrifice, who places wealth before him as the chief aim of his being, will soon cease to hesitate in regard to methods of securing it. If he cannot gain it by lawful industry, he will resort to fraud and deception, crime and woe. A large amount of the dishonesty of the present day, may be traced back to the love of money, and the unscrupulous means taken to secure it. Better be poor, than rich at the sacrifice of honesty. Better toil day and night, and eat the bread of poverty, than have a passion for gold which will corrupt the heart, canker the soul, and lead to the commission of foul and horrid crimes.

> " Oh cursed love of gold; when for thy sake
> The fool throws up his interest in both worlds;
> First starved in this, then damn'd in that to come.'

4. *They are brief as human life.* Were we on a journey through a strange country, and stopping here and there, only for a night, we should deem our accommodations of small importance; we should not think of fitting up in a costly manner, a house in which we should remain but a few hours. Human life is a journey through a strange land. Our home is beyond it, far away. Each object we behold is a monitor, pointing us downward to the grave in which our ashes will soon repose. Is it not vain, then, for us to give our whole attention to wealth and fame? We cannot carry them with us into the grave. The

10

rich and poor are alike in the coffin, and all the fame of earth will make no difference in the world to which we are hastening. I have read of a man who was rich on earth. He fared sumptuously every day. He was clothed with purple and fine linen. He rode in his chariot. He reveled in wealth and splendor. But death, the common enemy, visited his splendid abode, and hurried him away. He took no gold, no silver, with him. His chariot he left behind. His magnificence, pomp, and distinction, were all of the earth. In that other world, he was miserably poor. He had no home. On the waves of an angry sea his soul was tempest driven. He had no pillow but the wave of fire, and in vain he prayed for a cup of water to cool his parched tongue. I have read of another man, who sat at that same rich man's gate, full of sores, and covered with wounds. He was poor, *very poor*. But in time, he died. Angels caught his spirit, and carried it up to a world of bliss. All was changed. In an hour, he had become wealthy, honored, and supremely blest. There is an anecdote circulating widely in the papers of the day, which although old, so strikingly illustrates the vanity and brevity of wealth and fame, that I will give it in the language of another: "In the middle of the eleventh century, there arose a Mohammedan prince in Egypt, by the name of Saladin. Ascending the throne of the ancient Pharaohs, and guiding the Moslem armies, he rolled back the tide of European invasion, with which the Crusaders were inundating the holy land. His legislative genius constituted him the glory of his own country, while his military exploits inspired Christendom with the terror of his arms. The wealth of the Orient was in his lap, the fate of millions hung upon his lips, and one half of the world was at his disposal.

" At last death, the common conqueror of all, came to smite the crown from the brow, and to dash the sceptre of this mighty monarch. As he lay upon his dying bed, looking back upon the visions of earthly glory, fast flitting away, and looking forward into the impenetrable future, his soul was overwhelmed with those emotions which must under such circumstances, agitate the bosom of every thinking being. For a long time, his unbroken silence, indicated the deep absorption of his thoughts, by the new subjects which now engrossed his spirit. At last, rousing himself from his reverie, with that firm voice which ever was accustomed to be obeyed, he said: ' Prepare, and bring me my winding sheet.' It was immediately done, as commanded, and the winding sheet was unfolded before him. The dying Sultan gazed upon it, long and silently, and then added : ' Bring here the banner around which my chosen guards have rallied in my victories.' The banner was presented at the royal couch, and all in silence awaited the

further direction of the monarch. He paused a mo
ment, and said, ' Remove those silken folds, and at
tach to the staff in their stead, the winding sheet.'
It was done with the promptitude with which the
orders of the Sultan ever were obeyed. The dimmed
eye of the dying monarch gazed upon the mournful
emblem of mortality, as it hung from the staff around
which he had rallied his legions on the field of blood,
and added: ' Let the crier, accompanied by the musicians, in a funeral dirge, pass through all the streets
of Damascus, and at every corner, wave this banner
and proclaim, ' *This is all that remains to the mighty
Saladin !'*

" Then was there seen such a procession, as the
imperial city had never witnessed before. Gathered
in front of the portals of the palace were the musicians, the crier, with the strange banner, and the
military escort, doing homage to this memorial of
death. Silence pervaded the thronged city as the
wailings of the dirge floated mournfully through its
long streets   The crowds in silent awe gathered at
the corners. Suddenly the dirge dies away, and all
is still. The hearts of the people almost cease to
beat, as the cold white sheet, soon to enshroud their
monarch's limbs, is waved before them. Not a sound
disturbs the silent city, as the clear voice of the crier
proclaimed, ' *This is all that remains to the mighty
Saladin !'* Again the soul-moving strains of the re-

quiem vibrate through the air, and the procession moves along its melancholy way. As the stars came out at night, the spirit of the monarch took its flight, and the winding sheet enshrouded his limbs, still in death. Seven hundred years since that, have rolled away, and what now remains to the great monarch of the East? Not even a handful of dust can tell us, where was his sepulchre."

Look young friends, over the earth, and witness the pursuits of men. See how they chase the fantom shapes, which the god of this world sends, but to delude and destroy. They strive for fame. They dig for gold. And how long, think you, it will be, ere the *winding sheet* will be all that remains to each of them? Let them fill their coffers, let them secure the applause of the good and bad of earth, let them be all they wish to be, and the common conqueror will spoil the vision in an hour. How wise was that monarch, who employed a page to remind him, at certain hours every day, that he was but a man. Wherever he was, under whatever circumstances, surrounded by his court, in his study, or in the feast-chamber amid the revelers, the page whispered in his master's ear, " *Philip, thou art mortal.*"

Need *we* monitors to remind us of this? We have them. See you, that star, which twinkles and goes out; the sun which shines awhile, and sinks behind the western hills; the leaf which falls when autumn comes; the shuttle, the cloud, the dew. Daily, hourly, they whisper in our ears, "*Thou art mortal.*" And shall we heed the warning or not? Shall we give to Vanity, or God, our noble powers, our priceless time? Shall we strive to be honored with applause which will die away ere we have crumbled to pieces in the grave? Shall we be rich only in the treasures of one short fleeting life? Shall we be among those who despise honest toil, and imitate the man,

> " Who lord of millions, trembles for his store,
> And fears to give a farthing to the poor;
> Proclaims that penury will be his fate,
> And scowling, looks on charity with hate.

No, we have a higher calling. The acquisition of property is not the great end of our being. We have been formed to do good to others, and act a holy part in the reformation of mankind. Around this employment hovers a true dignity, gathers a real splendor. Riches are not forever, and the crown will not endure to all generations, but the glory of doing a kind and lovely act, will follow us beyond the sepulchre; and when wealth has crumbled around our tomb, and fame has died away along the shores of time, the solemn employments of this life will rise up to gladden the heart, and throw a charm over the pages of imperishable memory. Dig not into the bowels of the earth for that which is truly good, but look upward to thy God! With him all is pure, noble, wise, honorable, while all beneath the skies is vanity. The crown will fall from the monarch's head; the sceptre will drop from his palsied hand; the throne will crumble and decay; wealth will take to itself wings and fly away; all earth's greatness will perish, and the king, the pampered child of opulence, the learned philosopher, the senator, the priest, the gifted and the noble, must seek shelter in a narrow, dark, loathsome sepulchre. Death will stand unappalled before the man at whose word earth turned pale; he cares not for royal forms; he will not be bribed by wealth.

> "Earth's highest station ends in 'here he lies,'
> And dust to dust concludes her noblest song."

LECTURE VII.

GAMBLING.

Is not thy wickedness great? and thine iniquities infinite? For thou hast taken a pledge from thy brother for nought, and stripped the naked of their clothing. *Job*, xxii. 5, 6.

HATEVER may have been the peculiar significance of these words, as used by Eliphaz the Temanite, we shall find them no less appropriate when applied to gambling and the gambler. This vice, which I propose to make the subject of discourse·this evening, does indeed rob the naked of their clothing, and secures the pledge without rendering an equivalent. More effectively than intemperance, or slavery, or war, it cheats its victims, and destroys their souls. It is a system of polite robbery, genteel murder, and fashionable suicide. Gambling consists in receiving property without rendering a just equivalent. Every game of hazard, from the turning coppers of the ragged urchin by the wayside, to the stake of the hoary man, who lays his whole fortune upon the table, and risks it all; from the first cast of the novice, to the game by which the winner's coffers are filled in one hour, is gambling. From the insipid game of the jewelled female, to the carousal of the deformed, misshapen man; from the parlor, with its glittering lamps, its sweet music, and its lovely occupants, to the game played in the haunt of woe, where an old wheelbarrow answers for the table, and rude blocks for chairs, it is all gambling. Lottery prizes, betting, and the like contrivances to secure property without earning it, are all included in the list of gambling operations, and alike deserve the disapprobation of community.

I am well aware that many men who stand high in society, are engaged in this vice. I know that many buildings which rear their fronts proudly, in our large cities, have been erected or purchased with money thus obtained. I know that the stock of goods in many a store, is the product of this very crime. But does this fact change the nature of gambling? Not at all. Respectable men cannot make it a respectable vocation; gold has no transforming influence over it; silver cannot cover its hideousness; music cannot drown its wails of woe. Death clatters with the dice, and damnation stares out from the winner's card. All the efforts which are made to make this vice attractive to the virtuous portion of community, only renders it more disgusting and odious, gives it new features of hate and deception, and secures for it the name of fraud and corruption. Indeed, the law recognizes gambling as a crime, and in many places all its resorts and haunts, are closed by the officer of justice. And so it should be. There is no propriety in penetrating the cave of the midnight robber, the hovel of the forger, the den of the assassin, and dragging them away to the halls of justice, while the gambling saloons of our large cities are left to do their work of destruction, beggary, and death. There is no propriety in condemning and imprisoning the poor man, who in the urgency of the case, steals a loaf of bread to feed his starving wife and children, while gambling, which is a wholesale system of theft, is left to impoverish community and destroy the characters of our fellow-citizens. To induce you to loathe and abhor this vice, I will now offer upon it, a few remarks to which I request your attention.

1. *Gambling is a monstrous system of prodigality.* Money has its uses. Properly employed it is like time and education, a blessing. Rightly used, it enables us to do good and become extensively useful in the world around us. But if a man would waste a fortune, let him become a gambler. If he would in the shortest time, scatter the earnings of years, let him resort to the gay saloon, and engage in games of

chance, and drink in the dear delights of the gambler's purgatory. You have only to look around you,
and on every hand will present themselves to your
gaze, the wrecks of fortunes w' ich were once deemed
inexhaustible. You have only to go out into society
to find men who started life with thousands at command, but who have now no home, no fortune, no
happiness. The gambler inevitably becomes a ruined
man. He may win for a time, he may fill his purse
with his ill-gotten gains, but the unseen hand will
sweep them away, and leave him penniless. I know
that men begin to gamble with a very different
opinion. They want wealth, and deem the game of
chance the best method of securing it. They set sail
upon the sea of guilt with the idea of becoming rich
without labor or toil. But how sadly does experience
controvert this sentiment. Gambling, instead of being the royal road to fortune, proves to be the path
to houseless, homeless poverty. Instead of being the
flower-blooming way to affluence, it is found to be the
thorn-planted road to crime and disgrace. I am
aware that men are found here and there, who have
riches obtained by this crime. Some live and die, all
surrounded with the wealth thus gotten. But these
are the exceptions to the general principle, and form
no argument in favor of such crimes. God seems to
have forgotten them. He allows them to go on in
the work of accumulation, until they are as rich as

Dives, with hearts as hard and frozen as was his. Poverty, shame, wretchedness, are the almost universal results of gambling, and hundreds and thousands who have practised it, have found too late, their fatal mistake. Hence when we see a young man beginning to gamble, we may set him down as two-thirds ruined. If he be a merchant or a tradesman, you may expect erelong to hear of his failure. If he be a mechanic, or a lawyer, or a physician, you may calculate to find him ere many years are gone, in a mad-house, or a prison. You may depend upon his ruin with almost mathematical certainty. Like a fearful vortex, which swallows up every vessel which comes within the influence of its fatal circles, so gambling will swallow up every fortune upon which it can fix its gorgon eye, or lay its withering hand. Be not deceived! Think not that gold will fill thy purse! The home of gambling is the home of prodigality and poverty, where men who have been accustomed to roll in splendor, learn to feed on husks, and bite the dust of despair. If, therefore, you would avoid failure in business, poverty in your family, disgrace in society, and misery in hell, avoid the table of the gambler as you would the den of villany.

2. *Gambling excites, intoxicates, and maddens the brain.* The young man who is about entering upon the practice of the vice which we are discussing, supposes that he has perfect control over himself, and

can leave the table at any time, stay from it if he wishes, and return to it when he chooses. But this is not the case. The gambler is not his own man. When once he has entered the fatal path, he is impelled by an irresistible impulse. There is no stoping-place. Borne onward almost unconsciously, he loses command of himself, and with rapid strides hastens to his own ruin. Frequently, one night is sufficient to accomplish the work of destruction. Let us examine the process for a moment. A young man comes to our large cities from his distant home, with a few hundred dollars in his pocket. With the busy throng of living beings, he has no acquaintance. He spends his days in labor, and when night comes, sighs for some congenial spirits, with whom he may associate He wanders out to find them. The church is dark, and its doors are closed. The hall of science rears its front, but no living orator attracts the passing crowd. Everywhere, his ears are saluted with deep rumbling sounds, like distant thunder, and the lights streaming from the windows of the gay saloon, illuminate the night. He has read of gambling and crime. He has nowhere to go, and looks in to see if what he has heard is true. Once within the enchanted chamber, he is within the fatal circles of the tempter. In the foreground, he finds the card-players around their narrow table, and in the rear the bowling arrangement in full tide of operation Beside the former, he sits down. With intense interest he watches the play as it proceeds, and at length joins in it. Awhile the sharps allow him to win. This is a part of their infernal trade. He wins again and again. Now new visions flit before his mind. He has been accustomed to look upon wealth as the result of years of toil; now he can secure it, ere morning comes. His soul is on fire. He is dizzy with excitement. Already he fancies himself the owner of millions. By and by he stakes the whole sum which he brought with him, to invest in business. The practised villains see that it is no use to dally longer with him. They commence the game, and ere an hour is done, the young fool rises from the table, as poor as he was born into the world. He rushes to his boarding-place, in a state of mind more easily imagined than described. The next day beholds him pale and haggard, yet fearfully excited. He must win back what he has lost. He borrows all he can. and loses it. Soon he begins to steal. He does not mean to be a thief, but he must win his money back. The road to detection and imprisonment is short. A single year is often found sufficient to corrupt the purest mind, and leave a complete wreck of human character. The fearful excitement ruins both the body and the mind, and leaves a man, the fairest portrait of human misery. Think not, that *you* can pander with the vice and remain unharmed ! Think not.

that you can engage in it, and retire from its scenes, when you will! A few games will excite passions which no argument can subdue, no logic convince. The strongest mind will be turned by it, and the purest character, it will eventually ruin. The confirmed gambler presents us with a pitiable spectacle. His nerves all unstrung, in many cases his body crushed, and his look wild and fearful, and his mind like a disordered machine, racking and crushing itself to pieces, and spending its energies for its own destruction.

3. *Gambling is the highway to idleness.* Man was made for industry. • God has formed him for labor and toil. He has endowed him with powers of body and mind, which will fit him to accomplish much good in the few years of his earthly span. Moreover, God seems to have given us an aversion to idleness, and to the idler, and no person in the community, is so little respected as a lazy, indolent, young man. But gambling is the parent of idleness, and has been the means of converting many a well-disposed and industrious youth, into an idle, lazy vagabond. It first teaches the young man that labor is disreputable for men of wit and sense, that it will do well enough for slaves and ignorant persons, who have no skill and genius, that men of refined manners, and intelligent, polished habits, ought not to be required to dig, and tug, and strive. It next pro-

sents, the folly of working hard all day, and perhaps all night, for what can be secured in a single game. In this manner it takes the attention from pursuits of business and industry, and congregates its subjects in saloons and cellars, where they can play at night, and lounge, and smoke, and curse, and sleep, during the day. It creates an uneasiness, a fickleness, a discontent with one's employment and pursuits, and breaks up all regular business habits. It is not common for a professional gambler to be an industrious man. His trade is a kind of system of lazy vagabondage, and renders him physically, mentally, and morally unfit for any useful pursuit. Go into a gambling room in the daytime, and you will find a score of dissipated fellows congregated there. At a time, when the trader is in his store, the laborer at his toil, the mechanic in his workshop, these knights of the bar are engaged in lounging on cushioned seats, reading low publications, uttering blasphemous jokes, and drinking the sparkling wine, *like gentlemen.* Occasionally they will come forth to the light of day, looking like demons reeling up from the bottomless pit, and staggering to their homes, to abuse a wife, or dash to the earth a child, who comes to twine its little arms around the father's form. For the purpose of gambling, they have money enough, but for the wants of the family, to clothe the wife or feed the child, they have none. They will work all night casting the polished ball, but will shun the hammer as if it was a viper, the pen as if it was a fiery serpent. To just such an extent, as a man becomes a gambler, does he also become an idle, useless, lazy spendthrift. This is plain language, but as true as plain. All past experience and observation teach it, and you have only to follow out the gamblers in any community, to have it fully and painfully confirmed.

4. *Gambling is a system of falsehood.* Truth is one of the loveliest of the virtues. The man of truth is an estimable character. Truthfulness consists, not simply, in always avoiding direct falsehood, but in an upright, consistent course of action. There is the lie of the hand, as well as the lie of the lip. Sometimes a look conveys a lie; a shrug of the shoulders, or a shake of the finger consitute, not unfrequently, the greatest falsehoods. A man of truth is one, who is open in all his dealings; there will be no trickery, no double-dealing, no insinuations. His lips and his conduct will agree with each other. He will not be pleasant and fair in your presence, and plunge a dagger to your heart when your face is averted. He will not utter smooth compliments when you are listening, and when you are gone, sting your reputation with the poison of asps. Unused to deception, he will not suspect it in others, but will act towards his fellow-men on principles of open, candid honesty. But gambling is entirely opposed to truth. In itself, it is a lie, its

promises are hollow and deceptive, its pleasures false and fleeting. It is carried on by falsehood. From the very nature of the case, the gambler cannot be a man of truth. When he sits down to play, he sits down to lie; the play is a falsehood, and the gambler has forfeited his character for truth, to just the extent that he has become involved in the web-work of this vice. The skill exercised by the gambler is not like the skill of the lawyer, in an eloquent argument; not like the skill of the mechanic, who performs a difficult piece of work; not like the skill of the trader, who displays his goods to the best advantage. The *genius* of the gambler, is a genius for deception; his skill, is a skill to cheat. The very tendency of the crime is to unbend the character from its integrity, and lead up the young to crime of open and damning character. A gentleman of this congregation remarked to me awhile since, " that upon inquiry at one of our houses of reformation, it was found that nine-tenths of the boys who had been placed there, had been employed previous to their confinement, in tending and doing little errands, and setting up the pins, *for gentlemen*, in gambling saloons." These places not only corrupt the men who congregate in them, but they are training up a class of boys to dishonest and fraudulent practices, and making them at the outset of life, dishonest and corrupt.

5. *It is a system of wholesale theft.* I know that

it is not what is usually denominated theft, but though called by another name, it is no less really that crime. Without giving any equivalent, the property of another is appropriated to the use of the winner, and though the involuntary consent of the loser may be given, it is against his wishes and will. This the fortunate party knows, and when he sweeps the stakes into his own pockets, he has evidence that his opponent bitterly regrets it, and would keep his money, if he had the ability to win it back again. Notwithstanding this knowledge, the gambler will sit down to the table, and coolly win the last dollar which the hapless victim may possess. It may be said, that the loser is aware of all this, and ought not to play if he does not wish to lose. True, but should the maniac barter his farm away for a copper cent, or, the idiot sell his valuable house for a handful of silver; would the law, would public opinion justify the sharper who had made the bargain? Would not every honest man look upon this transaction of the villain, as base fraud and gross dishonesty? Would they not cry out against the wrong, and demand the punishment of the offender? Now the young man who is just beginning to gamble, is insane. He may have his reason on other subjects, but on this he is deluded and intoxicated. The mad excitement has turned his brain, and set his soul on fire. And thus he will continue, until like the professional gambler, his heart

is burnt to ashes, or petrified to flint. He will continue a monomaniac until conscience is gone.

And by what name shall we call the man, whose
soul is too dead to feel, and who deliberately sits
down to secure by trickery and deception, the money
of his excited, insane neighbor? What name shall
we give to the crime which he commits? Before
God, that man is a robber; his crime is robbery.
He appropriates to his own use, the property of
another, and gives him no equivalent. He wrongs
and abuses the poor dupe of his villany, and leaves
him without remorse, to hunger or thirst, live or die.

But the victim himself is not the only sufferer.
Frequently young men who have amiable and virtuous
families, practice this vice. They by some unfortunate combination of circumstances, become entangled
in the net of the seducer, and leaving their families
night after night, resort to the den of infamy, there
to win or lose, amid the fumes of brandy, and the
sound of cursing. Sometimes these young men lose
their all; they stake it in some unfortunate game,
and see it swept into the pockets of a competitor.
Enraged and drunken, each one returns to his family.
The children see him come, and cry for bread. The
wife points to her famishing little ones, and beseeches
him to secure them food. With all a woman's earnestness, she pleads for money enough to buy a single
garment to cover their freezing limbs. What shall

he tell her ?   What reply shall be given those hungry
children, as they cry for BREAD.   Why, that a god-
less wretch met him in the abodes of woe, and
wronged him, cheated him, robbed him of all; left
him a beggar, and sent him home without a shilling
in his pocket, *to see his children starve—their mother
die.*   The gambler who has won, has not stolen money
from the pocket of his victim only, but bread, *bread,*
BREAD, from the mouths of his wife and children.   If
a man comes into my house at night, and takes a single article, it may be a loaf of bread from the larder,
or an armful of wood from the pile, the officers of justice will pursue him, and if taken, he will suffer imprisonment.   But the gambler may steal the bread
from a hundred families, and leave them in the shivering time of winter without fire, without clothing,
without food, and yet he is allowed to walk the streets,
and move among men, as if he was as virtuous as an
angel.   You have only to converse with men who are
familiar with this subject, to learn that it is a wholesale system of theft and dishonesty.   Reformed gamblers will tell you tales of sorrow which will melt
your heart.   They will describe to you the strength,
the fearful power of the strange, unnatural excitement, when once it has obtained dominion.   They
will declare to you that family Bibles have been
pawned to secure money to play with ; that the
clothing of children, has in some cases, been stolen

from the wardrobe, and staked upon the issue of the game ; that the ring which was placed upon the finger of the wife, on the day of marriage, has been torn from her, and gambled away. A case occurred awhile since, within the limits of our own city, of this revolting character. Two little children had been clothed for the Sabbath School, by the hand of charity. Some, who now hear me, assisted in the work. Kind hands fitted and made the garments, and in due season the children appeared in the house of God. Three Sabbaths came and passed away. Ere the fourth had arrived, the father of those children took their warm, comfortable garments, and by relating a plausible story to one of his neighbors, succeeded in selling them. The money was taken to the saloon of a man who lives in affluence, and there lost in gambling. A few days after, I met the little boy in the street, and when questioned, he related to me the fact which I have now given, and which was subsequently confirmed by the mother, and even by the wretched father, with whom I had a conversation. Could I bring that little child, and induce him to tell you his tale of woe, as he told it to me, on the sidewalk of the bleak street, you would need no further appeal upon this subject.

6. *Gambling nullifies the marriage relation, and introduces disorder and confusion into families.* Home is the seat of domestic felicity. If home is

what it may be, and what it often is, the relatiors of husband and wife, parent and child, are full of sacred pleasure. If home is not what it should be, these relations will fail to confer that pleasure which God has ordained, and which under proper circumstances will proceed from them. Now one view at gambling will suffice to convince you, that it strikes a blow at domestic bliss. It allures the husband from his home until a late hour at night, and returns him to it, excited with wine, and maddened at his losses. In the saloon, and in the street, he dare not vent his rage, and he goes into his family, to the spot, which of all others, should be most free from harsh words and angry looks, there to act out what during the evening he has not ventured to develop. On his poor wife and child, the storm of his vengeance bursts with terrific fury, and threats and blows reply to the mild request for food and raiment. I scarcely know of a more fearful frame of mind, than that which the gambler has, as he returns to his family after a night of debauchery, his property gone, his head aching and throbbing, his heart bursting with its own anguish. His wife may receive him with kindness, his children, bright-eyed boys and girls may cluster around him as he enters, but he has no inclination to return their kindness, and he stalks through his dwelling, venting his indignation alike upon God and man.

7. *Gaming leads to intemperance.* Crime never

goes singly and alone. Seldom do we find a man, who lives in the habitual practice of one vice, and of no other. A man who will swear profanely, will generally cheat; if he will cheat, he will steal, and commit forgery; if he will do these deeds of darkness, he will gamble, get drunk, and perhaps, if occasion requires will commit murder. The same disposition and state of heart which leads to one of these crimes will, if not vigorously controlled, lead to the whole. Our sins are like the links of one great chain, and are to a considerable extent inseparable. Between gambling and intemperance, there is a direct connection. A man must drink, and become half drunken, ere he can play with skill; the wine-cup must sharpen his wits. Before he begins to drink, he is cautious, hesitates, and considers, ere he lays his money on the table. He plays with an unsteady hand, and thinks of home. The intoxicating cup must be used to drive away these feelings; to check the rising emotions of affection for his family; to drown the voice of reason, and make him desperate. Then when he is half drunken, when he has become half dead, he is fit to play; then can he pledge without hesitating, the bit of crust which his child must eat or starve; then can he stake the hat upon his head, the shoes upon his feet, the family Bible, and the family itself.

When the game is over, and the excitement has passed away, he must drink again to invigorate his system, to restore his energies, to quiet his nerves, and make his heart strong for another revel. This matter seems to be perfectly understood by the keepers of gambling houses. Hence, they always have a bar, at or near their den of crime. Gambling cannot be supported without drink, and we consequently find the saloon and the rum-shop, side by side. When the poor victim sees his hard earnings swept into the pockets of the practised villain with whom he plays, when he remembers his poor aged parents whom he is bound by every holy tie to support, conscience will begin to work, and if he has strength enough he will resolve to return to his home. At such a moment, the maddening bowl must be used. The beverage of hell must be placed to his lips, and in the excitement which it occasions, all holy thoughts, all sacred associations must be crowded out of sight, until his last dollar is staked, and the poor wretch is driven to madness, and perhaps to suicide.

8. *Gambling deadens the heart and destroys all kind and tender feelings.* Common, ordinary theft and dishonesty do not do this, to any such extent as gambling. A man may steal a purse from the pocket of a stranger, and yet love his family. He may cheat in business, defraud every customer, and return to his home with real affection. But a confirmed gambler, really loves no one, in heaven or on earth. Father, mother, brother, sister, wife, child,

are alike odious, and uncared for. The tender ties which bind other families in one holy band, are severed, and when gambling has become an absorbing passion, home has no attraction, and friends no influence.

It may be supposed, that I am using language stronger than the case will bear; that my views of gambling arise from an ignorance of the real feelings of those who are engaged in the practice of the vice. But if I am deceived, I am not alone in it. Some of our oldest, best, and most experienced men, have come to the same conclusion. The opinion of the virtuous community was expressed long ago, and gambling has been considered a crime, among Christians, ever since the days of our divine Saviour. In all ages it has had the same hardening, degrading tendency. In every clime it has been fraught with corruption and sorrow, and from the time when the murderers of Christ sat down beneath the cross, to gamble for his garments, until now, it has had the same tendency to corrupt human nature, and chill the heart to all lovely and pure emotions. That it may be seen that I am not alone in this opinion, let me introduce the statements of men of more age, wisdom, experience, and goodness, than myself, confirming the same statement. One writer* says, "The finished gambler has no heart; he would play at his brother's

* Rev. Dr. Nott.

funeral; he would gamble upon his mother's coffin." Another* declares that, "Gambling palsies the heart, and so effectually silences the voice of conscience, that a man can commit any crime and feel no remorse." Says another,† "Not long since, a young man acknowledged to me, in the greatest anguish of mind, that drinking and gambling, into both of which he fell in college, had almost accomplished his temporal and eternal ruin. There are, in every place of considerable size, fiends in human form, who are ever on the alert to entice young men into these practices, that they may increase their miserable gain by the destruction of soul and body." Another,‡ speaking of the gambler, says, "As he walks the streets, childhood should flee in terror at his approach; uncontaminated youth should hide from the very sight of him; the maiden—her brow now blanched with fear, and now suffused with indignation—should spurn him from her path; honest manhood should shrink from contact with the basest of the species; and old age, leaning on its staff, too feeble to turn aside for refuge, should lift its eyes to heaven, to be delivered from a contamination more foul than the grave. The gambler should be made to feel that he is a marked man; that in earth's homes, and in earth's hearts there is no place for him; that on his habitation

---

* Horace Walpole.   † Rev. William W Patton
‡ Rev. Joseph W. Thompson, D.D.

is written "*hell*," and on his brow is written "*fiend!*"

Another* says, "After hearing many of the scenes not unfamiliar to every gambler, I think Satan might be proud of their dealings, and look up to them with that deferential respect, with which one monster gazes upon a superior. There is not even the expectation of honesty. Some scullion-herald of iniquity decoys the unwary wretch into the secret room; he is tempted to drink; made confident by the specious simplicity of the game; allowed to win; and every lure, and bait, and blind is employed — then he is plucked to the skin by tricks which appear as fair as honesty itself. The robber avows *his* deed, does it openly; the gambler sneaks to the same result under skulking pretences. There is a frank way, and a mean way of doing a wicked thing. The gambler takes the meanest way of doing the dirtiest deed. The victim's own partner is sucking his blood; it is a league of sharpers to get his money at any rate; and the wickedness is so un-blushing, that it gives, at last, an instance of what the deceitful human heart, knavish as it is, is ashamed to try to cover or conceal; but confesses, with help-less honesty, that it is fraud, cheating, *stealing*, *rob bery*, and nothing else." The same writer elsewhere remarks, "When *playing* becomes desperate gam-bling, the heart is a hearth where all the fires of

* Rev. H. W. Beecher.

gentle feelings have smouldered to ashes; and a thorough-paced gamester could rattle dice in a charnel-house, and wrangle for his stakes amid murder, and pocket gold dripping with the blood of his own kindred."

I have but little more to say upon this topic. I hope I have convinced you of the folly of gambling, and led your minds to such an abhorrence of the crime, as will in after life, shield you, by God's blessing, from its terrific evils. I have used strong language, but not stronger than the subject demands; and if there are any present, who have become involved deeply in this passion, they can attest the truth of my statements. Go from this house to-night, my young friends, with a determined hostility to all gambling operations. Remember, that they are devised to steal your money, blast your character, and ruin your soul. Remember, that those who habitually assemble in saloons appropriated to these purposes, are generally knaves. As says the poet:

> " Whene'er the gaming-board is set,
> Two classes of mankind are met;
> But if we count the greedy race,
> The knaves fill up the greater space."

Beware, lest you be deceived. Gambling is a system of falsehood. It will promise you a fortune in an hour — wealth in abundance — happiness, without mixture of sorrow. But none of them, does it confer.

When the inquisition house, at Madrid, was destroyed by order of Napoleon, the commanding officer found an image of a beautiful virgin. The workmanship was most perfect, its proportions were correct, and beauty rested on each chiseled feature. This image was an instrument of torture. The victim was commanded to go up and embrace the virgin, and as he placed his bosom against the cold bosom of the statue, and his lips against the cold lips of the marble, a spring was touched, an internal machine was set in motion, and the arms of the virgin filled with sharp daggers, arose and encircled the poor sufferer, and cutting into his flesh, mangled him in a most horrid manner, and destroyed his life. Gambling is such an image. It looks well at a distance, but it is armed with knives which will cut, not only the body but the soul. Fly from the gambler's house, as from the door of death. Fly from the gambler himself. He will strive to ruin thee. Poison is in his heart, and falsehood on his tongue. He seeks thy ruin.

> "Beware of yonder dog;
> Look, when he fawns, he bites; and when he bites,
> His venom teeth will rankle to the death;
> Have not to do with him, beware of him,
> Sin, death, and hell, have set their marks on him
> And all their ministers attend him."

LECTURE VIII.

INTEMPERANCE.

At the last it biteth like a serpent, and stingeth like an adder. Prov-
erbs, xxiii. 32.

NTEMPERANCE, like other vices, is deceitful and seductive. It frequently presents a beautiful exterior, while within it
is all corruption, and as loathsome as a
sepulchre, full of dead men's bones. Youth is
charmed and cheated by it, and old age, it often
covers with shame and disgrace.

You have seen a calm cloud appear in the
heavens in a clear day in summer. At a distance
it looked beautiful. Its shining edges glittered
with delusive splendor, and it moved up the sky
as majestically as the chariot of Jehovah. As
it approached, the beauty disappeared; on man
below, it cast dark, threatening glances; the
golden fringes vomited forth forked lightning;
and what afar, seemed mellow music, was soon
found to be harsh and terrific thunder. Soon
the tempest was abroad on earth. The beasts

of the field fled for shelter to the shadow of the high rock; the yellow harvest of the husbandman was swept away, and man himself fled, a fugitive before the storm.

Intemperance is like that cloud! It promises shel ter and shade to the thirsty spirit, but soon bursts upon human life with all the fury of the tempest. It sends its blast and sweeps its tide, into the domestic retreat, across tribunals of justice, and up to the very altars of the church of God.

You have seen a serpent winding himself noiselessly through a bed of flowers, and anon lifting his crested head above the foliage, and sporting himself with many a gambol. You have admired his beauty, agility, and strength, and watched his movements with intense delight. Even the wild flowers which bloomed in his path, seemed to bend forward to kiss his beautiful form, and he in return moved aside, lest he should crush the fragile things, and scatter their tiny leaves. As you gazed, a mother and her child came on, and stooped to pluck those flowers. Then was the ferocious nature of the monster developed. Around those shrinking forms he coiled himself, and with a hissing sound struck them with his fangs. Crushed and wounded, the child and mother were left to die, while the splendid monster moved away, and was soon lost from view in the dense forest.

Intemperance is such a serpent! To youth it prosents a beautiful exterior. The wine sparkles in the cup, and the gay festival attracts the unthinking throng. "At last it biteth like a serpent, and stingeth like an adder." Within its coil the victim groans and writhes in agony, until the poison, like boiling blood, flows through all his veins, reaching his brain and setting his soul on fire.

You have seen the ocean calm and tranquil. As far as the eye could reach not a ruffle disturbed the surface of the waters. Like a sea of glass, it reflected the form of every bird which took passage over it, and gave back from its clear bosom, the polished beauty of the heavens above. Invited by the serenity of ocean and sky, the mariner launched his vessel, and spread his canvas to catch the gentle breeze. Soon a change came on. The wind blew like the hurricane. The waves tumbled and foamed upon each other. The ship plunged, and quivered, and strained in the trough of the sea. Sunken rocks now lifted their huge forms and sharp peaks high above the water, and anon were buried deep, by the mountain billow. Morning came; and a vessel, without mast, or rudder, or sail, or chart, or compass, or crew, floated upon the bosom of the surge.·

Intemperance is like that ocean! To the youthful voyager it seems as calm and placid, as a sea of glass.

But as he ventures out; as the green hills of so-briety disappear, the waves of destruction begin to

12

dash around him; the whistling blasts of poverty make frightful music; the moaning of the pitiless storm disturbs his dream of pleasure, and ere long he is tossing, an unmanageable wreck, upon the sea of temporal and eternal ruin. To point out the dangers of the sea of intemperance, and utter a solemn warning to the young, will be the object of the present discourse, and while I do this, I request your serious and candid attention.

I need not stop to prove that our young men need caution upon this point. Although the temperance reformation has laid its heavy blows upon the shivering sides of the dominion of king Alcohol, his throne is not yet overturned. His dark, infernal empire still stands. The frowning fortress from which he hurls firebrands, arrows, and death, still lifts its front in the midst of the Christian community, and on every side, are monuments of his dreadful conquests. True it is, that intemperance has been driven from the marriage festival, and the chamber of mourning; from the pulpit of the minister, and the bench of the judge; but unabashed, it has sought out other homes, and laid its snare for new victims. What then, we ask, are the solemn warnings which intemperance gives to young men?

1. *The drunkard shall come to poverty.* Poverty in itself, is not a crime. No disgrace belongs to the man, who by reverses in business, is led down from

affluence to destitution. The poorest man who walks this earth of sorrow, or who toils in vain to clothe and feed his children, can stand in the presence of the man of millions, with no consciousness of inferiority. But when poverty is the result of crime, it becomes at once sinful and disgraceful; when it is the result of gambling, or drinking, or lying, it covers its victim with a robe of shame. Under any circumstances it is exceedingly unpleasant and inconvenient to be *very* poor, and by most men, poverty is dreaded as one of the worst of evils. Now poverty is as sure to follow a course of intemperance, as light and heat to follow the rising of the sun. God has so ordained. In his word he has declared that the drunkard shall come to poverty, and wherever we behold drunkenness, we also gaze upon squalid misery. Go into any community and you will find affluence to be the result of sobriety, and destitution the sure attendant of dissipation. You will expect to find in the neat, vine-covered cottage, a frugal, temperate man; and in the hovel, unpainted and desolate, the windows shattered, the doors unhinged, an intemperate and dissipated man. So universal is this fact, that we expect a young man to ruin himself, squander his property, become idle and worthless, when he commences a course of intemperance. We predict with almost unerring certainty, that a few years will make him a pauper or a criminal, and leave him in a mad-house or prison, the vic-

tim of his crimes. The wretched beings, who sometimes reel along our streets, the sport of boyhood, and
the shame of manhood ; the miserable creatures, who
hide in cellars, and bar-rooms, and taverns, were once
as respectable as those who now walk the earth, with
proud step and lofty look. But forgetting the declaration of the Almighty, " the drunkard shall come to
poverty," they took the social glass, and drank its
contents. The pledge was disregarded, and the warnings of temperate men, unheeded. Step by step,
they descended from respectability and affluence to
wretchedness and woe. Property was wasted, and
character sacrificed. Self-respect took its flight, and
those who were once the enterprising, industrious,
hopeful young men of our country, are now the reeling, staggering inhabitants of dens and caves of infamy.

One such case, came under my own observation,
about one year ago. A young man, with whom I was
intimate in childhood, became intemperate. When a
boy, he had a generous heart, and a noble disposition.
We all loved him, and of our circle, he was the pride
and ornament. Friends looked to him, with the
highest anticipations of his future usefulness. When
at a proper age, he commenced business, and for
awhile was exceedingly prosperous. The little property, which he had at first, increased, and he was
looking forward to wealth and affluence. In an un-

fortunate hour, he learned to drink the social glass, and drain the maddening bowl. Kind friends hung around him, and presented their remonstrances; the church of which he was a member, uttered its kindest warnings; an aged mother hung upon his steps with prayers and tears. Heedless of them all, he clung to his boon companions, and his cups. "I shall never become a drunkard," he said, "I can control my appetite; your fears are vain." Soon business was neglected. The little fortune which he had accumulated was scattered to the blast, and discouraged and disheartened, he became a drunkard. The associates of his early days stood aloof; the church, with many tears, and after many fruitless efforts to reform him, withdrew the hand of fellowship; his mother died of a broken heart, and the young man himself, mortified and ashamed, fled from the scenes of his youth, and the companions of his childhood.

One morning, about a year since, a messenger called at my door, and asked me to visit a young man in distress. Amid the peltings of the pitiless storm, I hastened to the place where he was. I found the street, the house — if house, the wretched tenement could be called. Up into the third story, I traveled, amid dirt and filth, and entered the chamber to which I was directed. In a cold room, on a bed of straw, covered with a single moth-eaten blanket, burning with fever, tortured with rheumatism, and delirious with drink, was stretched a young man. I could not recognize his countenance, or recall a single feature. "I do not know you," I said to him. He cast on me a look of agony, and replied: "Good God, has intemperance blotted out my manliness, and made me so much a demon, that my early associates do not know me?" Then he covered his face, and wept aloud.

His story is soon told. He was the young man, who in early life had given such promise of usefulness. To one degree after another in his fatal habit he had advanced, until his money was gone, and he was a pauper. To our city he had wandered in search of employment, and here I found him, in the condition which I have described, with both feet frozen, and none to minister to his wants. In the wretched dwelling, and among the more wretched occupants, he found no sympathy. He learned in all the bitterness of his spirit, that the drunkard will come to poverty.

I would not affirm, that every case of intemperance will end like this, or that the destruction of every intemperate young man, will be as speedy and as awful. But sooner or later, poverty will crush the spirits of every man who "looketh upon the wine when it is red," or who goeth after strong drink. He may bear up against it for awhile, but it will ultimately overthrow him. It will perplex and disturb his business; it will mortgage his house, and his farm; it will place an attachment upon his stocks; it will ruin all his prospects for this life, and the life to come.

2. *Intemperance ruins the physical constitution.* In the creation of the body, God has displayed infinite wisdom. More wonderful than any complicated work of human hands, it bears the impress of divinity. It is fearfully and wonderfully made, and is a specimen of workmanship, unrivaled in the arts. The Maker of man did not form him thus fearfully, in order that he might be broken by disease, and crushed by vice. He made him upright. He stamped the blush of health upon his cheek, and sent him forth to look upon the earth beneath his feet, and the heavens above his head.

You have seen a beautiful machine, fulfilling the purpose of its maker, and working with order, regularity and harmony. You have examined it closely, and admired the perfection of all its parts. You have complimented the skill of the artizan, and deemed his work, one of extraordinary ingenuity. You have also seen that machine disarranged; the order and harmony of its movements gone, and entirely incapable of performing the work for which the maker designed it.

The human body under the influence of intemperance, is like that disarranged and broken instrument. The purpose of its creation is defeated, and it becomes the seat of numberless diseases, aches and pains, sorrows and woes, for which God never has intended it. The drunkard presents a fearful specimen of a broken-down man. From the head to the feet, he is covered with disease. He moves along the street, with downcast eyes, or staggers to and fro, with heavy tread; his nerves are all unstrung, or braced beyond endurance; his head aches and throbs; his bloated face spoils the beauty of a human being; his knees totter and smite against each other; his livid lips are closed over teeth decayed; his swollen tongue prevents his ready utterance; his idiotic look, betokens speedy death; his eye glares at one time, and is languid and bloodshot at another; and his brain is racked with a thousand fancies, and agonized by a thousand fears. Go search earth's darkest caves, and bring up to the blaze of day, the inmates of your prisons and dungeons; your insane asylums and madhouses, and none will you find so miserable and degraded, so lost to all that makes up a perfect man, as the victim of intemperance. Take some case within the limits of your own observation; some friend who tampered with the terrible destroyer, and been ruined. You knew him perhaps, when no shade of crime had passed over his manly countenance; when he walked with his head erect, and his bosom bared to the storms of life; when life flashed from his eye, and vigor was in his step; when the stranger noted his manly form, and correct deportment. You have seen that form bend, not with age; you have seen that step falter, not from fear, and that once noble form reeling from the drunkard's purgatory, to lie besotted and beast-like by the wayside. You have seen everything noble and beautiful in this God-made body, utterly spoiled; the divinity in man crushed out of him, and the temple of the immortal soul laid in ruins. Nor will the young men whom I address to-night, avoid this terrible destruction of the human system, if they enter the fatal avenues which lead to the drunkard's fate. They may suppose that they have power to drink, or refrain from drinking. They may boast how strong they are, and how easily they can dash the inebriating cup to the earth. But their boasts are idle as the wind. The great army of drunkards with crippled limb, limping form, bleeding heart, and maddened brain, thousands of whom die every year, utter their notes of warning. The broken, diseased, death-struck forms of prostrate men, as they lie along the path of life, give fearful admonition. The opening graves, into which the remains of men are tumbled after they have cursed themselves and all around them; graves on which the flowers seem unwilling to bloom, and over which the birds appear to sing in sadness; graves wet by no widow's tears, consecrated by no orphan's lament; graves which angels shun, or by which they weep in sorrow, as on their mission of mercy, they pass through the city of the dead, all sound the alarm, and by the dumb elo- quence of their speechless harmony, bid the living throng, beware of the drunkard's hopeless doom. You remember the famous dream or vision of a dis- tinguished clergyman, for the publication of which, he was beaten in the street and imprisoned. The scene was said to be in Deacon Giles's Distillery. The dreamer saw the demon-workmen at their unhallowed employment, manufacturing with great zeal the elixir of death. He heard their ferocious and blasphemous expressions. While he gazed on, barrel after barrel of the accursed poison was drawn from the cistern and prepared for sale. The employment of one or more of the fiends was, to mark and label these bar- rels and hogsheads of rum and gin, which had been put up. Quenching a coal of fire in the liquid which he had made, the infernal monster went to work. On all the barrels, in letters which would remain invisible until the first glass was drawn, and then burn forth like fire, he wrote, " consumption," " palsy," " fe- ver," " plague," " insanity," " madness," " redness of eyes," " sorrow of heart," " death," " damnation," and the like expressions, which, when the liquid death had been sold, and the buyers drew from it for the first time, flashed out in the faces of the thirsty cus- tomers, who stood waiting around the bar. With fearful consternation they saw written in words of flame, the diseases which they knew were preying upon their systems, and fled from the place in terror.

What that dreamer saw in vision, we behold an existing fact. Though on the barrels in the rum-shops, we do not find the words of fire written there by demon hands, yet we behold more fearful inscriptions on the living, dying countenances of men who walk our streets. Gleaming forth from fiery eyes; seen on the wan and haggard cheek; read in the stooping forms and staggering tread; heard in the hollow cough; felt in the aching head, and beating heart, proving to us that intemperance

> " Is palsy, plague, and fever,
> And madness all combined,"

are the fearful inscriptions of death and damnation.

3. *Intemperance poisons domestic felicity.* The sacredness of HOME has often been made the subject of discourse. Scarcely a man now hears me, whose heart has not beat quickly, at the mention of the endearing word. HOME — it is associated with all the pleasant scenes of childhood and youth; with the names of companions, whose countenances are now forgotten; with the prayers of parents and the love and kindness of brothers and sisters, who are now sleeping in the grave. Nor, until human nature be changed, will this love of home be entirely destroyed.

Men who wander far away, over ocean and land, who journey from clime to clime, as fugitives and wanderers, look back with pleasant emotions to a spot which they call their "home." But intemperance, like gambling, is calculated to corrupt home, poison its joys, and wither its flowers. Many a family has been made wretched and miserable by intemperance. The fire on many a hearth has been put out, by the drink of death. Indeed, intemperance so transforms a man's character, that he is not prepared to fulfill the relations which exist between him and his family. However kind he may be when sober, however he may provide for the wants of his family, if he is an intemperate man, he cannot be a good husband, or a good father. The thing is impossible. Drink transforms the kind and indulgent sire into the harsh, unjust, and cruel tyrant. Men, who when sober are affectionate and pleasant, become under the influence of inebriation, fierce and wicked.

Awhile since, I became acquainted with a family, the head of which was a kind, inoffensive man, who loved his wife and his children with a pure affection. He was one of those peculiar men whose hearts are full of kindness for all around. He was, to some extent, an intemperate man, and when drunken was the very reverse of what he was in his sober moments. On one occasion he returned to his home in a state of intoxication, and for awhile sat brooding by the fire, silent and stupid. Soon his son came in, a little, bright, intelligent boy of six years. The child at school had received the commendation of his teacher, and in his joy had hastened home to repeat the words of kindness to his parent. Somewhat boisterously he rushed into the room, and with eyes glistening with delight, threw himself into the father's arms. That brutal sire, changed from friend to fiend, uttered a fearful oath, threw the child from him, struck him in the face, and dashed him to the earth. What other acts of violence he would have committed we know not. The mother seized her child, the blood gushing from his nose and mouth, two of his teeth gone, and fled with him to the house of a neighbor. When reason returned, had that father committed murder, he could not have been more penitent. He cursed his cups, and yet clung to them. He cursed the man who sold him drink, and still hung about his workshop of death. He wept and prayed over his child, and still continued in the habit which caused the injury.

Not long ago, the papers of our city gave us an account of a murder committed in our very midst. A husband, who in his sober moments was kind to his companion, in a fit of intemperance, had destroyed her life, and sent her spirit to the bar of God. Notwithstanding his vow to be her support and protection, he caused her death. With his own hands he beat and mangled her form, until the vital principle was gone, and then retired to bed, to sleep the drunkard's sleep, and dream the drunkard's dream.

Southern papers, awhile since, gave an account too dreadful almost to be believed. A newly married couple had lived together, for a short time, in quiet and happiness. Soon after the marriage, the husband began to drink. The fatal habit rapidly increased upon him, and in two years, he was a miserable drunkard. One night he returned home at a late hour, and found his wife in a flood of tears. With an oath, he commanded her to dry her cheeks. She could not. Tears had been her meat, day and night, and they came unbidden. She ventured to remonstrate. Seven devils seemed to enter into him. He struck her to the floor; with a sharp knife he gashed her flesh, and hacked her limbs, and leaving her half dead, fled away. In the morning friends came in, and found the wife insensible, and her babe playing in the purple flood, and when they uttered exclamations of horror, the child held up its hands, covered with a mother's blood, and wept.

I have introduced these cases, that I may ask, if man is bad enough, with all his depraved powers and passions, to accomplish deeds like these, without the aid of reason-robbing drink ? No ; crushed as human nature is by sin, it needs some artificial stimulant to bring it up to a point, where it can sever so recklessly the dearest ties of nature, and commit crimes, at which cruelty itself revolts. And we find intoxicating drink, furnishing just the excitement which is required to induce husbands to imbrue their hands in the blood of their wives, and fathers to destroy the lives of their children. We find intemperance leading to family disturbances and social discord. We find it to be the cause of sorrow in households, and divisions between companions who have lived pleasantly for years.

4. *Intemperance impairs the intellect, and produces idiocy and madness.* There is a strong sympathy between the physical and mental parts of man. One acts upon the other. If the body is diseased, the mind is also found to be in an unhealthy condition. If the mind is unhinged or thrown from its balance, the body suffers accordingly. The intellectual is more valuable than the physical. It will endure when the body has decayed, and will continue to be, after the material structure has disappeared. Now intemperance acts directly upon the mind itself, and indirectly through the medium of the physical constitution. The injury done to mind by this vice, is beyond all calculation. Men of strong and vigorous intellect have been bowed by it; shining talents have been dimmed and tarnished, and the fairest prospects of intellectual greatness blasted by its fatal influence. The legal and medical professions, and

even the ministry, have lost some of their brightest ornaments, and been robbed of some of their choicest jewels, to gratify the lust of this accursed Moloch. Memory now recalls the form and countenance of one, who a few years since, bid fair to stand among the first orators at the bar. His professional services were held in high estimation; as an orator he was enthusiastically applauded; as a profound scholar, an able statesman, a clear and vivid writer, he had but few superiors. The political party of which he was a member, nominated him for a seat in Congress, and but for the fatal habit of intemperance, he would have been elected. But all the hopes of his youth were to be disappointed. The love of strong drink grew upon him; he was seen in a state of intoxication in the court-room; confidence in him was soon lost, and now if you will visit the city of his birth, you will find the wreck of the once polished lawyer and accomplished statesman. His once powerful intellect is shattered, and although he was, but a few years since, the pride and admiration of the bar, he dares not now attempt an argument in open court. A hundred other cases equally plain and pitiable might be produced. The history of intemperance is full of them, and on every page of its fearful record can be found the names of men, who have fallen from the highest summit of intellectual greatness, to the lowest depths of degradation and infamy. The ravages of intemperance in its last stages, are fearful indeed. The mind becomes entirely overthrown, and loses all power of self-control. Like a ship without rudder, or chart, or compass, it plunges on the terrible waters of a deep, dark sea. He who would see the intellect entirely dethroned, and hell begun on earth, must visit the bed of a man suffering with the torment of *delirium tremens*. The poor sufferer is haunted by every image of terror, he sees horrid shapes, he hears horrid sounds. Images, which no mortal man ever conceived of before, start up, and throng around him. Satan with all his legions come racing up from pandemonium to hold their infernal conclave in his chamber ; beside his dying bed. Ghosts of murdered men drag their bleeding bodies from the grave, and lay them at his feet. He sees — he hears — he feels everything dreadful. Each figure on the wall, becomes a fiend, which looks upon him with glaring eye ; the friends who move about the room in tearful silence, are to his disordered fancy, pale spectres, who cry avaunt, and shake at him their long, bony fingers ; the blanket which covers him, he imagines to be a huge snarl of snakes and reptiles woven together, and feasting on each other. Inconceivable terror takes possession of him ; he starts from his bed in anguish ; he bids the fiends begone, and hears only their mockery. He utters heart-rending cries, which echo far down the street at midnight ; he pleads with his physician to tear the strangling serpents from his throat, to drive away the demons, who have come to torment him before his time.

In what prison or mad-house, can you find insanity like this ? · In what lone cell, or daɪĸ chamber, can you find madness which equals that of the dying drunkard ?   In the darkest secrets of human misery the *delirium tremens* has no counterpart, and as a source of unspeakable anguish, and unmitigated misery, it stands alone, unrivalled by anything this side of perdition.

A few months ago, a virtuous, amiable young man, was bitten by a mad dog, and awhile afterwards died of hydrophobia.   In the arms of that terrible disease, the hapless victim lived a few hours in excruciating torment, pleading with his friends to give him some drug which would destroy life.   The fearful news spread rapidly from one to another ; for awhile this awful disease was the subject of conversation in all circles ; the press uttered its warning, and the pulpit made use of the solemn providence.   All were alarm-. ed ; cities framed laws, and the great commonwealth made the disease the subject of solemn legislation. Muzzles and chains were used ; dogdom was in terror, and hundreds of these creatures have been destroyed.   All this is well — I would not have it otherwise.   I only ask that the madness of intemperance may receive a like attention.   In the whole history of a city, but one case of hydrophobia has occurred — but one death from the fearful malady, and yet the town is all agog; editors are writing, ministers are preaching, and lawyers are pleading, that something be done, while the madness of inte. nperance — a disease infinitely more to be dreaded than the hydrophobia, is destroying its victims every month, and no one seems to be alarmed.

Suppose you, a man should build houses on the corners of every street, that from their doors and windows, he might let loose upon the unthinking populace, mad dogs of every size and tribe, to bite the people, and spread the poison of disease throughout the whole community; what would be thought of him? Why, the law would lay its heavy hand upon his murderous vocation, close his doors, and drag him to some place of confinement. And here are men found on almost every street whose sole business is, to let loose upon society insanity and madness in their worst forms, who send their *rum dogs*, mad as Satan, to bite with venomed tooth the loveliest members of our families, whose trade is, to spread among men, the worst kind of hydrophobia, and make war alike upon the bodies and the souls of our fellow-creatures.

5. *No drunkard shall inherit the kingdom of God.* This is the solemn declaration of an inspired penman. And how reasonable its truth! The kingdom of God is a place or state of purity. We are informed that

there, shall be heard no discordant clamor; no voice
of wrangling and bitterness; no sound of disorder,
tumult and wrong. There, all is pure, all is lovely,
all is holy. There angels sing, and holy beings make
sweet music to God a ad the Lamb. Gathered there
from every clime, are the holy men of earth; men
who have toiled and suffered in this world, having no
abiding place below the skies. There is no night
there — no tears — no sorrow. One deep, wide wave
of glory and delight, submerges all. And can the
drunkard expect to live in such a world? Can he
whose lips have so long given utterance to blasphemy,
attune them to the melody of heaven? No; the word
of God declares the thing to be impossible. The
drunkard's voice would make a discordant sound in
the world of bliss. His shout would burst like a wail
of despair upon the startled inhabitants of the celes-
tial abode, and contrasting his own deformed and
crime-blasted character with the purity and bliss
around him, he would find heaven to be more intolerable than the deepest pit in hell. And where shall
the poor drunkard go? He has misery and suffering
on the earth, and where shall he go? Look upon him
as in his chamber, in the last stages of *delirium tremens*, he is held upon the bed by strong hands; see
his wild and horror-struck countenance; hear his terrible, blasphemous expressions; gaze upon his rolling
eye, and behold his consternation as he imagines that

his room is filled with snakes and devils; and tell me, where shall he go?

One word more, and I will close. In all large cities, young men are exposed to numberless temptations. On every side are the snares of the enemy, and from the gay saloon with its glittering ornaments, to the low hovel of wretched inebriation, are found the sources of intemperance and vice. Beside the open and known resorts of infamy, are secret dens and caves in which the wicked hide themselves, and into which the young are decoyed and ruined. A friend, a few days since, entered one of the most public buildings in one of our cities, and came to the door of a room which refused him entrance. He discovered a secret spring, and touched it. The door flew open, and he saw in full operation the bar, and the gaming-table. Congregated there in the broad day, and yet concealed from human view, were the wretched beings who make crime a pastime and sin a recreation. And other such places there are in all our large cities, whose sole object is the destruction of the young. To these facts it is worse than madness to blind our eyes. They meet us on every hand; they stare us in the face at every turn we take.

Young men, it devolves on you to say what shall be the future history of the temperance reformation. It devolves on you to say how far the burning waves of intemperance shall sweep on, and where they shall be stayed. I therefore call upon you, in the name of our common humanity, to arise in all the vigor of youth, and manliness, and arrest, if possible, the tide of ruin which is sweeping over the beauty of our land. We need warm hearts and willing hands. The monster with whom we have to contend, is more powerful than kings and emperors, and will not be defeated without a struggle. Come then to the work of humanity; the work of God. It will ultimately triumph, and intemperance will be driven from the world. We may toil long against the evil, but victory will eventually crown our labors. It is the cause of human happiness, and would reflect glory upon the angels of God, were they permitted to engage in it. Be not discouraged, though little may seem to be effected.

"Never doubt a righteous cause;
  Go ahead!
Throw yourself completely in;
Conscience shaping all your laws,
Manfully through thick and thin,
  Go ahead!
Do not ask who'll go with you;
  Go ahead!
Numbers? spurn the coward's plea!
If there be but one or two,
Single handed though it be,
  Go ahead!
Though before you mountains rise,
  Go ahead!
Scale them? certainly you can:

Let them proudly dare the skies;
What are mountains to a man ?
Go ahead !
Though fierce waters round you dash,
Go ahead !
Let no hardship baffle you :
Though the heavens roar and flash,
Still undaunted, firm, and true.
Go ahead !"*

Invoke the assistance of " God o'erhead," and do your duty well, and when the course of life is run, and the last hour of human probation arrives, you will look back upon your efforts to stay the tide of crime, and save the drunkard from temporal and eternal destruction, with high and holy satisfaction. Angels will whisper in your ear of men redeemed from vice and crime, and by your hand plucked as brands from the burning. Such tidings will be sweeter music to your worn spirit, than all the anthems of the earth, and though borne upon the blast, or wafted on the gentle breeze, the flourish of trumpets, or the melody of the organ, mav disturb the silence of your death-chamber, the memory of your good act, will kneel by your dying couch, and do its homage there, and breathe upon you a sweeter strain than can be purchased by the wealth, the honors, the noisy pomp and parade of empires.

* George A. Light.

LECTURE IX.

Be sure your sin will find you out. *Numbers*, xxxii. 23.

IN is generally committed with the hope and prospect of concealment. Did the criminal believe that he should be detected and punished, he would be deterred from the practices which have ruined so many of the young men of our land. Did the prospect of discovery and disgrace rise up before every one who goes forth to the commission of iniquity, hundreds would start back as from a horrid vision, and shun crime as a thing of fearful character. When men go forth to steal, they pass along with noiseless tread, and cautiously find their way to the golden treasure. They endeavor to erase every sign of their crime, and leave their own reputation stainless. The ideas of detection and disgrace, if they ever enter the mind, are driven out, and the criminal looks forward to enjoyment and not detection; to impunity, and not punishment. He knows that he *may* be overtaken, that he *may* be exposed, but the certainty that he *will* be exposed, does not seem to enter his mind.

The midnight murderer hopes that his crime will be concealed forever. His motto is, " Dead men tell no tales;" and when the voice of his victim is hushed in death, when his tongue has ceased to move, he imagines that his dreadful deed will be covered up from all human scrutiny. He often moves through life, with his head erect. He converses about the murder which he has committed as freely as if he was innocent. Sometimes such persons will even allow themselves to be put on committees of investigation, and in all possible ways seek to blind the eyes of the community.

Thus is it with all criminals, of less or greater magnitude. They attempt to shut every door which would seem to be an inlet of light, and hope that the crime which they have done, will be buried up forever. But how vain is such a hope ! The declaration of the " Holy One," is, " There is nothing covered which shall not be revealed ; neither hid, which shall not be known." The murderer may do his deed of blood in the darkness of the darkest night; the robber may meet his victim, miles from any human habitation, and bury the body of him whom he has robbed in the leaves of the forest, or sink it in the channel of the stream; the pirate may wash his decks with the waves of ocean, and erase from his sails every spot of blood; he may murder the whole crew; he may burn and sink the vessel of his victims; but in all these cases, the crimes will be made known. Darkness, and distance from human beings, and the moanings of the pathless ocean, will not cover or conceal the tokens of guilt. The ground will spout forth the blood; the earth will disgorge the buried bodies; and the ocean will bear them scarred, gashed, and lifeless, to the shore, where the dead hand shall lie pointing ocean-ward, as if seeking the detection of the assassin.

Of course I am not speaking to a congregation of robbers or murderers. I am not preaching to those whose hands are red with blood, and whose consciences are corrupted and corroded with stains of awful crime. But I am speaking to a company of sinners; to a congregation of men and women who have all been involved in guilt, and who notwithstanding their many virtues are, to some extent, chargeable with wrong. If all are sinners, it is not unjust to suppose, that many have sins which they are endeavoring to conceal; sins which they would not wish to have known, even to their dearest friends. I think the purest man that ever walked this earth of ours, would hardly wish to have all his thoughts and feelings laid open before the world. There are so many wicked thoughts, desires, and deeds, hovering around human life, that the noblest and the best would shrink from an investigation. Nor is it unreasonable to suppose, that among so large a crowd of young men as throng our cities, there are those who have entered some of the fatal avenues of guilt, and are hiding it from their friends, and from the public gaze. It is not unreasonable to believe, that some have allowed unholy thoughts to manifest themselves in unholy conduct. There may be amid this throng, some one who has learned to love the music of the gambler's voice; who has begun to sip the poison-cup of inebriation; who lives in violation of the holy Sabbath, and who profanes the name of God, without hesitancy. To lead such to renounce sin, and avoid crime, I wish to urge several considerations connected with the detection of every transgressor.

I. THE STRONG PROBABILITY. The probabilities that sin will be detected, are confined to this life. In infinite wisdom God has so arranged the great drama of a changing world; so contrived its shifting scenes, that crimes are discovered when most we desire and expect concealment, and there is a strong probability that the vicious will be detected and exposed. These probabilities are,

1. *The confessions of associates.* In wrong courses and in crimes, men generally have some assistants and accomplices. They seldom go alone to commit

deeds of darkness and madness. They choose asso
ciates resembling themselves in moral character, and
to them impart their secrets, and unfold their purposes. They make their companions acquainted with
all their views and feelings, and thus place their lives
in the hands of others. Now there is a strong probability that these associates will reveal the secret and
expose the sin. Bad men do not long remain in company without strife, and the very person to whom
the knowledge of the crime has been communicated,
becomes the source of information and exposure.
How often do we hear of crimes thus exposed. Long
buried, and covered from human gaze, the criminal
has rejoiced in the prospect of everlasting conceal
ment, when lo! his accomplice, the sharer of the
spoils, the partner of his guilt, becomes his accuser.
The crime long forgotten is uncovered, the author
of it is branded with disgrace, and the scene ends in
misery and sorrow. Indeed, so common is the confession of associates, that we all expect crime to be
detected. When the tidings of murder, or robbery,
or wrong of any kind, are running through the coun
try, we watch the next daily paper to see the name
of the criminal, and learn his fate. We feel confident
that he will not escape ; that some voice will whisper
words in secret, which shall be spoken upon house-
tops, and those words such as shall make condemnation certain. The horrid murder which was commit-

ted beneath the walls of Waterville College, tho solemn tones of which have echoed far and wide over our land, and produced sadness in many circles, was exposed by one to whom the unfortunate physi‑ cian, who committed the crime, looked to for conceal‑ ment and confidence. The very man who was to bury the body, and hide forever all traces of guilt, was the one on whom the law relied to prove the crime, and fasten it upon one who stood high in the esteem and confidence of the people, and who was rising rapidly to eminence in his profession.*

2. *The power of memory.* It would be well for every criminal, to forget his own crimes. Could this be the case, detection would be much less certain, as far as this life is concerned. The man who has been guilty of some crime will frequently act in a suspi‑ cious manner. He will exhibit signs of guilt, when none around him suspect him of being involved in crime. He will dream at night, and start up with words upon his lips, which he would not care to have uttered. He will shun his fellow-men lest they see the agony of his heart depicted upon his countenance.

* Since this lecture was delivered, the providence of God has unfolded another diabolical attempt to murder on the part of C———. A plan deeply laid has been discovered when ready to be put in execution, and the life of an innocent man saved; while the foul murderer, foiled by a superior wisdom, and baffled by tho Almighty, has rushed up to meet his Maker, uncalled and unbid‑ den, a melancholy suicide.

He will show to those around him, that something is working upon his mind, and preying upon his heart. It is not seldom that the power of memory, by keeping the fact before the mind of the criminal himself, will betray him, and well would it be for every man who has done wrong, if he could blot the memory of the fact, as well as the fact itself, from the tablets of the heart, on which it stands recorded. But this can not be the case. The lamp of memory will burn ·as long as the soul of man endures ; it will stream its lurid light over every act of guilt, and forever flame with fearful intensity. It is supposed that nothing can be lost to memory ; that every act of life is treasured up ; that every thought which flits through the mind, and every word which escapes from the lips, makes an indelible impression. Though at times other objects may engross the attention, and sometimes we may lose entirely all recollection of what has passed, yet, sooner or later, memory will bring it up again. From her chambers where they have been concealed, but not destroyed, will past crimes start forth and hang like coals of fire, upon the conscience and the heart. I have been told by those who have fallen from high places, or crushed in whirling machinery and exposed to sudden, instant death, that in a space of time inconceivably short, the whole life was presented. Deeds long forgotten and buried out of sight ; words whose sounds long since had perish·

ed ; thoughts which had not been cherisned for years, came rushing across the mind, and in an instant thronged before the mental vision with startling accuracy. In the instant of time which was required by the ponderous wheel to turn with crushing force, the whole of this life, and a fearful view of the next, were given, and an age of misery endured in a single moment of time. Nor will the powers of memory ever fail; as each age of the future expires, and wave after wave of eternal duration sinks back upon the shores of the past, memory will be gaining more fearful power over those who have made earth the theatre of crime. This awful power constitutes the mirror of the soul, which grows brighter from every impression made upon it. It will contribute essentially to develop crime, and uncover deeds of dark ness, which all the ingenuity of the criminal has been unable to hide. It will expose to the public gaze, men who have long and fondly hoped for perfect security, and lay open to the hand of justice, and the ministers of the law, the criminals who have enjoyed their ill-gotten gains in fancied security.

3. *The upbraidings of conscience.* Conscience is the voice of God in the human soul. It is a principle implanted by the Almighty, within the bosom of every human being, to teach him what is right and what is wrong. When a man performs that which is acceptable to God, conscience will approve, and when he

violates the law of God, this faithful monitor will utter its admonition and speak out its condemnation. The power of conscience, of remorse, is great; and the most remarkable instances are on record, in which conscience has led the criminal to betray himself and confess, not only to God, but to man, the wrong which he has committed. I remember having heard of a man who in early life, was induced to rob his own father, by which the poor man was brought to bankruptcy and death. The son enjoyed his treasure for awhile, but conscience was busy at work upon his mind. His crime, his fearful crime, was continually before him. True, he did not fear detection. He had buried all traces of his deed so deeply, that he supposed no person could find it out, but his own unnatural conduct was a greater source of trouble, than all the fears of discovery. To drive away these feelings, he left the scenes of his infancy and childhood; plunged into business; buried himself up in the cares of the world, and in every way possible, endeavored to drown the voice which uttered its ceaseless upbraidings. But every attempt proved to be a failure. The form of his aged sire, as he went down to the grave, wronged of his property, and sorrow-stricken, was before his mind. He heard one voice — he saw one object — he felt one pang. It was the voice, the reproach, the condemnation of conscience. Twenty years rolled away, and his misery had become so great, that he came forward and confessed his crime. To the members of his own family, some of whom had been born since the wrong was committed, he unfolded the story, and then gave himself up to the officers of justice. I doubt not, there are some in every community who suffer from the reproaches of conscience. Concealed crime festers on the heart, and produces a wound which no hand can heal. Under the power and influence of this terrible attendant, the most aggravated crimes have been confessed and punished. Murderers and robbers, seducers and forgers, have come forward, and without hesitancy declared their guilt, and asked of the courts of justice, the sentence of the law. The deed, forgotten by all but the criminal, has been told, and the miserable one himself has desired punishment, as the only means of relieving his conscience of its torturing load of sorrow.

4. *The providences of God.* In a most wonderful manner, the providences of God work out his designs. When we contemplate the way in which the Almighty deals with his creatures, we are surprised. At first, there appears to be no order, no design, no harmony, in all his mysterious workings. The law of confusion reigns among men, and we can see but little order in the system of divine providence. But as we gaze, and study; as we watch the unfolding plan and purpose; as we learn more of God and his ways, we are surprised more at the order and harmony, than we

14

previously had been at the apparent disorder and confusion. We find the whole system of divine operations to be regulated by an unerring hand, and controled and governed by almighty power. We see the plan of God opened, and rendered successful. Providences which have been as dark as midnight, are now illustrated and made to show forth the praise of God, and surprising order is seen in all the wise arrangements.

In the most mysterious manner does the providence of God sometimes expose crime. A train of events which no human being could have set in operation, leads to the most startling developments, and criminals who have eluded the pursuit, and even the observation and suspicion of a most vigilant police, are discovered and punished, after all hope of detection had died out. The most trifling circumstances will be connected with a series of events which develop and bring to light, deeds which have for years been buried from all human scrutiny. The singular movements of some domestic animals; the words written upon the wadding of some discharged gun; the caving in of banks, in the sand of which dead bodies have been buried, and other things as trivial, lead to the detection of men who suppose they have concealed all tokens of guilt in the graves of their victims. And this providence will assist in the detection of all other criminals of smaller or greater guilt.

God is pledged against sin ; he abhors crime, and is resolutely determined to punish all who commit it. His providence, like a key, will unlock the secrets of darkness, and like a skilful hand, will unravel the thread of life, and expose when least we expect it, its follies and crimes. Nor can the sinner control these mysterious workings of the divine mind and purpose. What we may deem best calculated to hide, conceal, and cover up our sins, may be the very thing which shall expose our faults, and bring shame and disgrace. Letters written and disguised ; remarks made to direct attention to another quarter ; weapons thrown into the bushes by the wayside, all, instead of proving innocence, become proofs of guilt, and are used for a purpose the reverse of which was intended. It is related of an eminent clergyman, that on one occasion while walking in a graveyard, he saw the sexton throwing up the bones of a human being. He took the skull in his hands, and on examination, saw a nail sticking into the temple. He drew it out, placed it in his pocket, and asked the sexton whose skull it was. On receiving the necessary information he went to the house of the widow, and entered into conversation with her. He asked her, of what disease her husband died, and while she was giving an answer, drew the nail from his vest, and asked her if she ever saw it before. Struck with horror at the unexpected question, the wretched woman confessed that she murdered her husband; that her own hand had driven the nail into his temple.

5. *The bed of death.* Hundreds of persons pass through life unpunished, and though surrounded by observers escape detection, until they come to the bed of death. Hundreds, when they arrive at the last hour of probation, and stand on the outward boundary of life, are compelled by the awful circumstances in which they find themselves, to unburden their souls of the crimes which may have rested there for years, and which now come up from the deep retreats of memory to sting and poison, like venomous serpents. It does a sin-agonized spirit good to confess, and the dying hour has extorted many a tale of blood, shame, and folly, from the wretched man whose crime, like a fire shut up in his bones, has been concealed only that it may be revealed at last, under circumstances of greater awfulness.

Go to the death-bed of the wicked man, and you will hear him bewailing his sin. All his life, has his heart been growing harder and harder, until like steel it resisted every impression, but in an hour it is now dissolved. His lips have never been attuned to the simple melody of confession or prayer; but now one ceaseless stream of confession pours from him. This sin and that, this folly and that, rises up before him, and he asks forgiveness of God and man. Indeed, the soul seldom dares rush into eternity with a weight of sin crushing it down. The dying man would make clean breast, and do all that confession can do to make the burden less.

To such a death-bed scene will every unrepentant sinner come; such broken confessions will be the language of every heart which is not renewed and changed by God.

Thus far I have spoken of the detection of sin, as probable. The probability is very strong, as most criminals find it. But there is another view of the subject; a stronger and more fearful view, to which I will turn your attention.

II. THE AWFUL CERTAINTY. The language of Scripture, the caution which it gives to all, is, " Be SURE your sins will find you out." " For there is nothing covered which shall not be revealed, neither hid which shall not be known." On this point, the Bible leaves no chance for doubt, no opportunity to cavil or dispute. All sin shall be revealed. Committed in the darkest night, or in the brightest day; in the desert solitude, or in the crowded city; with or without associates; by man or woman; by angel or demon — it will not escape notice — it will not avoid condemnation and punishment.

1. *Because every sin is seen by God.* This is one of the most fearful considerations which can be presented to the mind of the sinner. God sees him. The eye which never slumbers, has watched all his

movements; detected all his faults, and beheld all his sins. He may have concealed them from father and mother, wife and child; on earth no mortal may tread, who has the least suspicion of what he has done, and yet all is known. God's eye has been fixed upon the deed, and he knew it all. Darkness, secrecy, and deception, have been unable to hide it from his view. This terrible conviction seemed to press upon the mind of David, when he exclaimed, "Whither shall I go from thy presence, whither shall I flee from thy Spirit. Thou art in heaven; thou art in hell; thou art in the uttermost parts of the earth. Darkness hideth not from thee; light is ever around thee; the night shineth as the day."

With the same propriety every sinner may use this language, and apply it to his own case; God is everywhere. He sees and knows all things, and understands even the thoughts of his creatures. It is in vain that an attempt is made to conceal our sins from his notice, or hide them from his gaze. He saw our first parents, when in the bowers of Eden they ate the forbidden fruit; he saw Cain, when with wicked hand, he smote his brother, and slew him; he saw the sins of the old world, which was before the flood; he saw the sins of his own people, the Jews; and as surely does he see, mark, condemn and punish our sins. Hide them from the minions of the law; hide them from the good and holy; hide them from loved friends and hated foes, and yet you cannot hide them from the eye of God. Piercing down through the realms of space, the awful scrutiny of the Infinite One is fixed upon us all, and as soon can we fly from our own existence, as from the gaze of Jehovah.

2. *All sin will be revealed at the day of judgment.* We are informed in the inspired word, that a record of all the deeds of men is kept; that in a book of remembrance, all the good and evil actions of life are recorded. What that book of remembrance is, matters not to us. The great fact that our accumulating sins are all to be treasured up, and at last exposed, is a terrible one. None but a man whose heart is hard, or whose mind is darkened by sin, could reflect upon it, without serious forebodings. Nor are the circumstances under which this revelation is to be made, calculated to remove, in the least, the sorrow of such an occurrence. We are led to believe that it will take place at the hour when all men, from all climes have assembled before God; when the world which we now inhabit, and which has been increasing in the splendor of its towns, towers, and temples, for ages, is all wrapped in the flames of the last conflagration, when the moon has turned to blood, and the sun has gone out in darkness, and the stars have fallen, like worlds of fire, from their courses on high; when the clouds are rolled together as a scroll; when

from their long resting-places, the dead are starting
forth to life and immortality; when the righteous
shall be shouting notes of glory and singing anthems
of deliverance, and the wicked are howling in the
madness of despair; when has come,

> "A scene that yields
> A louder tempest, and more dreadful fields;
> The world alarmed, both earth and heaven overthrown,
> And gasping Nature's last tremendous groan;
> Death's ancient sceptre broke, the teeming tomb,
> The Righteous Judge, and man's eternal doom."

At such an hour, and under such fearful circumstances, will the array of crimes which we have committed, present themselves before our bewildered
minds. In that solemn assembly will they be read
in the hearing of the whole intelligent universe.
Then will parents learn for the first time, what have
been the lives of their children; then will children
see how many errors clustered around the lives of parents; then will wives and husbands, brothers and
sisters, learn of each other what they never dreamed
or imagined before, and the secrets of all hearts shall
be made known.

I well know that with many persons, the idea of a
future judgment is rejected as absurd and ridiculous.
Not a few indulge in open sport with the solemn
things which are connected with it, and even churches
are erected, and pulpits built, and men set apart, to

silence the fears which the Bible gives in regard to it. And yet, as true as there is a God, and that God is the author of his own inspired word, the hour of judgment will come. Though long delayed by the goodness and mercy of God, the hour will come. The trumpet of the archangel will startle the living throng, and awaken the pale nations of the dead. The great white throne will be erected; the righteous and the wicked will be separated, and the winding up of all things will come.

And now, I ask, in view of all that has been said this evening; in view of all the solemn considerations which I have presented, should not the young cease from crime and learn to do well? If in this life, there is a strong probability, and in the life to come, a positive certainty, that sin will be detected, and if detected, punished, should not those who are engaged in practices which they know to be wrong, forsake them? The declaration of God is, " Whoso covereth his sins shall not prosper," and this declaration has been found to be true in all ages of the world. Crime may prosper for awhile, the wicked man may spread himself like a green bay-tree, and grow tall in his iniquity, but erelong the hand of God will be laid upon him; his dishonesty and criminality will be exposed to the gaze of justice, and his hopes and prospects of success will wither away.

The all-seeing eye of God is fixed on each of us.

Our hearts, our secret thoughts, are known to Him. We could not if we would, hide a single feeling, a single motive, a single desire. What folly then, to commit sin! Darkness and night cannot hide it; it will be exposed. And let the impression rest on our minds as we separate this evening, that the wicked, the vile, the abandoned, the murderer, the robber, the adulterer, are not to be judged alone. The members of this congregation will stand with the gathered millions, who come from all the ages of the past to receive their reward, or hear their doom. On that awful day, let me inquire, where according to your present character, you will stand?

> "When Thou my righteous Judge shalt come
> To take thy ransomed people home,
> Shall I among them stand?
> Shall such a worthless worm as I,
> Who sometimes am afraid to die,
> Be found at thy right hand?"

LECTURE X.

Wherewith shall a young man cleanse his way? By taking heed thereto according to thy word. *Psalm*, cxix. 9.

THE question proposed is of considerable importance, and gathers greatness whenever we contemplate the duties and dangers of young people. Situated as they are in life, and exposed to its trials and temptations, they need an infallible guide, an unerring counsellor. With no such guide and counsellor, impelled by the impetuosity and inexperience of youth, our young men will leave the beaten paths to success and greatness, and wander about in the wilderness of disappointment. No judicious mariner would enter a dangerous harbor for the first time, or sail up a river which has sunk thousands of vessels, without a pilot. However he might control his vessel while out upon the broad ocean, he would fear lest his ship should strike on some hidden rock, or some concealed bar, and go to pieces, while his skill would avail nothing. Hence, when he arrived at the entrance of such a harbor, or the mouth of such a river, he would discharge his cannon, and hoist his signals, that the pilot might know of his arrival, and come to guide him into port. The young man needs a guide over the ocean of life, as much as the sailor needs a pilot through the dangerous passage, or up the rocky river. And where can such a guide, such a pilot, over life's sea be found ? The Bible alone presents a perfect standard of human character, and a perfect guide for man under all circumstances of life. Inspired by God, and written out by holy men, it contains no errors, and admits of no mistakes; it prescribes with great distinctness the duties and obligations of the aged and the young; it will preserve the way of the youthful traveler, to his journey's end ; it will elevate the mind, improve the heart, and give gladness to the spirit.

You will, therefore, allow me to recommend the Bible to young men,

I. As a perfect guide in relation to the duties of life. The duties devolving upon us in this life, are numerous and important. The relations which we sustain to others, place us under obligation, and this obligation is nowhere so clearly delineated, as in the word of inspiration. Of importance is it, that we understand what we owe to others, and what they owe to us. A duty imperfectly understood, will be imperfectly performed, and if we have no guide on subjects of such magnitude, we shall make many mistakes and errors.

1. The Bible teaches the young man his duty to *himself*. It is the duty of every young man to be intelligent, virtuous, and respectable. In our days, immorality and ignorance are without excuse, and the man who is found with a depraved heart, and a beclouded mind is not only unfortunate, but guilty. There was a time when man could be ignorant without sin, but in the centre of the flood of light and information which is poured upon the world, ignorance becomes a sin, and is in the highest degree disgraceful to all who are found in its fetters. This the Bible teaches, and we are commanded to secure wisdom and knowledge, and ample opportunity is given us in the works of nature which are spread out, and the sources of information within our reach. Most persons suppose the Bible requires of us, nothing in regard to literary and scientific attainments ; that we can be wise or ignorant at our own option ; but this is a mistake. Mind, intelligent mind, is one of God's most precious gifts to man, and he demands of us the full improvement of it.

The cultivation of self-respect is also enjoined by the Bible, and certain principles are established, by the observance of which, a young man may respect

himself, and secure the approbation of all good men.
Every person is under obligation so to live, that he
can look upon his own conduct and character with
feelings of respect, and not shame and mortification.
The Bible does, indeed, forbid our estimating ourselves more highly than we ought to do, forbids our
attaching an undue importance to our own works, but
it nowhere forbids self-respect, nowhere discourages a
laudable attempt to secure the well wishes of others.
There is a conscious dignity of character, differing
from pride and selfish esteem, which is one of the
safeguards of youth.   It gives a feeling of manliness,
and enables its possessor to repel the assaults of temptation and sin, and stand erect amid descending tor-
rents of abuse, supported by the fact that he has a
reputation to sustain, a character to lose or keep.

The pursuit of happiness is also required by the
Bible.   The avenues which lead to it, are all laid
open to the youthful seeker, and he can enter them
and secure the prize.   The Bible instead of forbid-
ding, enjoins the pursuit of pleasure in any reasonable way.   It gives permission, even to the Christian,
to secure wealth, honor, health, and friends, in a
proper manner, and to a proper extent.   It only condemns and prohibits the inordinate and destructive
pursuit of things in themselves valuable, but rendered
worthless by being too eagerly pursued, and too fondly loved.   With its unerring wisdom, the word of God

has drawn the line between all that is good and all that is evil, and pointed us to one, and lifted up its voice against the other. The young man will appeal in vain to the heathen philosophy, to the philosophy (so-called) of our own times, to the example of the wisest and best men who have ever lived on earth, and find in them all, no perfect model for his imitation, no perfect guide to lead him on to success and happiness. But in God's inspired volume, he will have a faultless instructor, an unerring counsellor, an unfailing guide.

2. The Bible teaches the young man his duty to his *kindred* and *friends*. "Honor thy father and thy mother," is one of the ten commandments which were given with smoke and flame on Sinai. "Children obey your parents," is the reiteration of that sublime command, given under the more gentle light of the new dispensation. The Old and New Testaments alike inculcate the duties which we owe to those who have brought us into being, and guided us up through infancy and youth to manhood and womanhood. The good Book has many a precept, enjoining kindness to our aged parents, and unlike all the forms of heathen worship, which look upon the aged as worthless to society, requires us to love and cherish those whose heads are white, and whose limbs are feeble. It gives on this subject no uncertain sound, but brands the man who forsakes his father and mother, and

treats them with cold neglect, or cruel unkindness, as one of the most degraded of the race.

It teaches also the duties which devolve upon the husband and the wife. The relations which exist between these parties, have been misunderstood in all ages. In past times, the best of men have not duly appreciated the God-appointed institution of marriage, and when it has been entered into, its duties have been shamefully disregarded. Everywhere but under the light of Christianity, woman has been degraded from her true position, denied that standing for which she was intended by her Creator, and made to toil out her life in ignominious servitude. The Bible and volumes founded upon it, are the only books of morals which confer upon woman her real rights, and place her by the side of man as his equal. The Bible alone commands the husband to love the wife, and support and cherish her. Other systems of morality, agree with the Bible in enjoining obedience upon her, but leave the husband to act the tyrant at his will. But the Bible while prescribing her duties, makes his plain also; commands him to be kind and affectionate, and leave father and mother and cleave to her.

The Bible is also a guide in the management of children. By this book their support is placed upon the father, and he who refuses to supply the wants of his own family, is said to be worse than an infidel. How children should be educated and governed, the rules which should control parental authority, are all laid down, and were these rules·obeyed, we should not so often be called to bewail the conduct of wicked children. If instead of unlimited indulgence, the chastening rod was oftener used ; if instead of being blinded to all the faults, and alive only to the virtues of the children, parents would, or could look upon them, as others see them, and have an eye open to their vices as well as their virtues, they might save themselves many an hour of tears and lamentation. If instead of abusing their children with blows one minute, and smothering them with kisses the next, making fearful threatenings one day, and unreasonable promises the next, parents would comply with the plain and obvious teachings of Scripture,.they and their children would be far happier. Many of the best and kindest parents among us, are educating their children for prisons, almshouses, and scaffolds; bringing them up to manhood with passions unbridled, temper ungoverned and ungovernable, and moral principles but half cultivated. Could such parents look forward to the future, and see what would transpire after they are laid in the grave, or perhaps before that time, could they see their children wretched and miserable, on account of the indulgence of youth, they would be appaled, and start back as from a vision of despair.

3. The Bible teaches the young man his duties to

15

his *fellow-men.* By the wise decree and arrange ment of God, man is made dependent upon his fellow-man. The king on his throne is as dependent as the slave who kneels at his feet, and the boast of freedom and independence, in a strict sense, is idle. Nations are dependent upon each other. America and Europe, are somewhat dependent upon poor, downcast Africa, and superstitious, unenlightened Asia; and the nation which should attempt to live without the assistance of any other nation, would soon fall into barbarism. Much of our food and clothing come from other climes, and should we discard all but our own productions, we should return to the ignorance and degradation of our aboriginal inhabitants. Individuals are as dependent upon each other, as are nations. If we were equal, independent of each other, who would manufacture the fabric of which our dresses are made? who would build our houses? who would brave ocean to bring our food from afar? who would dig our canals, build our railroads and steamboats, and provide for the wants of the masses of society? Under such a state we should see each man building his own house, weaving his own dress, cooking his own food, spreading his own blanket, and living entirely for himself. The sick would have no watcher, no kind hand to smooth the pillow and fan the throbbing temples, and the dying would lie in unburied ghastliness. But God in his infinite wisdom has otherwise or dained. He has made us mutually dependent on each other, and placed in each human bosom a monitor, which recognizes this state of things, and impels us to fashion our lives accordingly.

Now the Bible clearly and distinctly makes known to us the duty which we owe to others around us. It does not leave us in darkness on such a subject, but points out the line of conduct which as parts of a great brotherhood we are bound to pursue. The Bible recognizes each man as a brother and friend. It admits certain distinctions of condition, but not of fact; admits a superiority in intellect, in property, in physical strength, but not in blood, and bones, and heart; admits a superiority in life, in progress, in thought, and being, but not in birth, or in death. One man is king, another is a beggar; one is a philosopher, another is an unlettered slave; one is a man of honor, another is a man of ignominy and shame, but they are all brothers; the king, the slave, the philosopher, the pauper, the man of honor, and the man of disgrace, are *brothers*. This the Bible teaches, and on this relationship depend certain duties which the inspired writers have stated for our instruction. Towards all men the great duties of kindness and forbearance are inculcated, and instead of the old threadbare maxim, " Might makes right," we have given us the golden rule, " Do unto others, as you would that others should do unto you." Inspired with this spirit the early believers in the Bible went everywhere preaching the word ; the missionaries of our times have labored, preached, suffered, and died, making sacrifices for the good of others ; the house of desolation and poverty, has been cheered, and the tearful eye of the mourner, upturned to God ; human society has been transformed, and the most desert places of the world, made to blossom as the rose, beneath its divine influence. Whatever is good and excellent, lovely and pure, and heavenly in human intercourse, we owe to the gospel of the Son of God.

4. The Bible teaches the young man his duty to *government*. In the times of the Saviour, the Jewish nation was wearing the Roman yoke. The people were ruled with an iron hand, and made to pay heavy taxes to support the splendor and pomp of the imperial monarchs. They justly deemed this taxation, this iron rule, oppressive, and frequently rebelled and raised an insurrection against the tyrants. On one occasion, a penny was brought to Christ, bearing the image and device of Rome. " Is it lawful to give tribute to Cæsar, or not ?" they asked. The reply of Christ is full of wisdom, prudence, and consistency. " Render unto Cæsar, those things that are Cæsar's, and unto God the things that are God's."

He here plainly inculcates the duty of obedience to the existing government. The Saviour doubtless shared in the opinion generally entertained by the Jews, of

the injustice of Roman tyranny, but while they were
living under that government, enjoying its protection, sharing its honors, they were bound to support
it.   While they were protected and defended by the
armies of Rome, they were bound to obey the laws
of Rome.   In other places, the sacred writers refer
to the example of Christ, in proof of his obedience to
law and order.   We do not find him inciting insur-
rections, or raising mobs and armies, but everywhere
teaching submission to civil authority.

Prayer for governments and rulers is enjoined upon
all Christians, and the great duties of *man as a citizen* are recognized throughout the whole inspired
word.   A distinguished writer* upon this subject
says: " When men unite in the establishment of a
government, they mutually promise, in all their relations with each other, to yield obedience to certain
fundamental principles.   The object of these principles is, to define and limit the power of the magistracy,
and to prescribe the manner in which this power shall
be exerted.   The enunciation of these principles
forms what is called a constitution.   This being once
established, it binds all, and it protects all.   It is a
solemn and mutual contract between every individual
on the one part, and the whole community on the
other part.   Upon the fulfilment of this contract, depends the freedom of every individual, and the secu·

* President Wayland.

rity of his rights, whether civil or religious. We can neither assume powers not conferred upon us by this instrument, nor refuse to carry its provisions into practice, either ourselves or by our agents, without a violation of our solemn obligations. It matters not how overpowering the majority by whom the outrage is committed, nor how small the minority whose rights are infringed, nor how elevated the position of the functionary by whom the act is performed. It is a crime of the deepest dye, and merits and should meet the sternest reprobation of every virtuous man. If, then, such be the responsibility assumed by every citizen of a free government, it surely becomes him to understand the provisions of that instrument, by which this responsibility is created."

5. The Bible teaches the young man his *duty to God*. There is no other book which authoritatively establishes the principles, on which as the creatures of God, we are governed. In fact, all we know of God with any degree of certainty, is drawn from the inspired volume. We may discern something from the book of nature, but the inscription is dim, and we are liable to make fearful mistakes. The whole heathen world have nature in all its most beautiful forms, and day by day, they study it, but does it make them wise? does it lead them to right results? Not at all. Instead of worshipping the great Jehovah, they adore the sun, moon, and stars, and

bow in worship before the creature instead of the Creator. From nature men may learn that the "Great Spirit" is good, but the delightful and truthful views of Divinity we have, could never be learned from the singing bird or the waving forest. High mountains, broad plains, and sandy deserts, have no voice to tell of Him who made them, beyond the bare fact of his power and might.

But the Bible reveals God in his true character, as the Father, Saviour, and Sanctifier of his people. It also marks out the duty of man, proclaims the necessity of unqualified submission, and having proved him a sinner, demands his acquiescence in the way of salvation through a crucified substitute.

The first great duty which is revealed, we find to be, full and perfect obedience to the law of God. This is required on every page of the sacred statute-book, and man is under obligation to give exact and impartial conformance to the decrees of the high chancery of the universe. Obedience or death, is written on every provision of the law of Moses, as with a pen of fire.

The second duty to God consists in entire submission to all the dispensations of divine providence. These are sometimes adverse and dark. We fail to behold in them, the wisdom or the goodness of the Being who directs and controls them. As they come upon us, one by one, we are apt to forget the character of Him who has dealt with us, in such an awful manner. But the Bible enjoins implicit submission to these solemn exhibitions of the divine character. It shows us how good God is, even in the midst of our sorrows; how kindness is blended with the blow which falls upon the wayward child of earth.

> " God moves in a mysterious way,
> His wonders to perform ;
> He plants His footsteps in the sea,
> And rides upon the storm."

Directed by this book, the mourner will ascend the mount of vision, and look forth upon the glorious scene which faith presents. His little sorrow will lie at his feet, while he, with uncomplaining voice, lifts up his heart to Him,

> " Who doeth all things well."

The third great duty to God, is faith in his Son. Perfect obedience is required, but never has been given in one single instance by mere human beings. Christ alone is sinless on the records of a sinful world. All others are involved in the great transgression. Hence faith in a crucified Saviour has been enjoined, and the nature and object of this faith are declared nowhere else. The wisest of the ancients, never thought of such a mode of saving sinners, and had the world been without a revelation from God, the great idea contained in the cross, would never have been known.

From the brief, hasty, imperfect view, which I have given of the Bible, as a book delineating the duties of men, we see its value and importance. Without it, man would have been enveloped in gross darkness, but now he stands in the sunlight of the gospel. The young man who makes the Bible the guide of his youth, need not mistake any path of duty and safety. That blessed book will teach him to be honest, temperate, frugal, industrious, truthful, and pious. It will make him a good citizen, a faithful friend, a prudent counsellor, a wise law-maker, a benevolent philanthropist, a steadfast, humble, faithful Christian. From the Bible as a guide in all matters of duty, we turn to the same book,

II. As a perfect guide in all cases of danger. Age has experience. The man of hoary head and bending form, has seen much of life. He has had dealings with the stern realities which gather around the pilgrimage of earth, and is, to some extent, prepared to grapple with the dangers which attend every human existence. But youth is without even this narrow and insufficient safeguard. It has no experience of its own, and is liable to run into danger, as well as mistake the path of duty. Experience makes us cautious. The aged approach every doubtful object with hesitating steps, and measure the distance before them, ere they advance. But youth sees no danger, and fears no disappointment. The young man dreams of pleasant fields, sweet flowers, gentle streams, green meadows, glittering waterfalls, and cloudless days. That life has deserts, high rock-ribbed mountains, deep and dark ravines, quicksands, and intricate fastnesses, he does not seem to realize.

You have seen a picture of some city. It was a beautiful engraving, and well proved the skill of the artist. In that picture you might have seen high towers, gorgeous dwellings, splendid temples, long streets well laid out, and rendered beauti-ful by waving trees and blooming flowers. Such a picture makes an impression upon your mind, and your reflections upon that city are of the most plea-sant character. Years roll on and you visit the place, and find yourself sadly disappointed. The artist had presented all that was beautiful, and con-cealed all that was hateful and odious. True, all that he had represented on his picture is there, and more besides. The tall stately spire, surmount-ing an elegant temple is there; but when the sun goes down, that tapering finger casts its shadow along a narrow, filthy street, in which the plague would be ashamed to make its home, or the swine to roam. The massive tower is there; but it has none of the beauty with which the skill of the artist adorned it The long streets are there, and they are very long but instead of beauty appears deformity. All is noise and confusion, and the traveler turns from it to his own quiet home.

Young people look at *the picture* of life, and see all its beauties, while defects are concealed, and consequently when they go forth and gaze upon reality, they are disappointed as much as is the traveler while visiting the city of which I have spoken. At a distance all is grand and gorgeous as the picture of a nation's capitol, but when we enter the winding avenues of society, we find them as odious and dangerous as the winding, crime-frequented lanes and streets of some of the most depraved cities. The disappointment which ensues, causes thousands to become vicious and dissolute. They find dangers where they only dreamed of safety, and are bewildered and amazed. The Bible, if carefully studied, and strictly obeyed, will prove a safeguard against all such dangers, and lead the young man through life, with no loss of character or happiness.

> "It is the polar star
> That guides the pilgrim's way
> Directs his wanderings from afar
> To realms of endless day;
> It points the course where'er he roam,
> And safely leads the pilgrim home."

1. The Bible will save young men from *dangerous error.* These are days of religious error. While sci-

ence is advancing, and rendering herself more secure, while men are settling down on true and sound principles, while the laws which control the heaven above, and the earth beneath, are becoming better known, while scientific truth has few opposers, and error few advocates, it is true as strange, that religious errors are multiplying, and twining themselves with serpent-like subtlety around the affections of the people. There is scarcely a doctrine of the Bible which has not been denied, and, to some extent, revelation has been shorn of its beauty and dignity. From the un-blushing infidel, who boldly affirms that the idea of God is a fable, the Bible all a lie of practised de-ceivers, to the erratic but sincere seeker for truth, who, while he believes the Bible, interprets it *as he understands it*, and attempts to narrow down the sub-lime objects of faith, to the grasp of human intellect, and refuses to admit any truth which is above the comprehension of mere human reason. The world is full of books teaching doctrines as false as the Bible is true; absurd, as truth is plausible; dangerous, as the way of life is safe. Attracted by the outward adornment of error, the young receive as truth that which the Bible denounces as falsehood, and cling to forms of deception, fearfully ruinous to the immortal soul. The framers of erroneous dogmas have adapted their systems and creeds, to meet and take advantage of the weakness and frailty of humanity. They have advanced sentiments which appeal to depraved man, and bend to his carnal inclinations. They hesitate not to say to the vicious and degraded criminal, " Thou shalt not surely die." They calm the fears of the wanderer from God, and by scattering a few artificial flowers in his path, make him believe he is on the road to heaven. Their systems are like splendid tombs in groves of cinnamon and orange.

Not long ago, I saw a splendid sarcophagus in a retreat away from the world's noise and confusion. The white marble, the overhanging willow, the skilful chiseling, the beautiful inscription, the calm tranquillity of the spot, and the mournful associations connected with it, all added melancholy interest to the resting-place of the dead. So beautiful was the external appearance of the charnel-house, that an experienced critic would scarce detect the slightest fault, and long after he had left the spot, the skill of that work of art would linger in the memory of the stranger. By and by, a stern and swarthy man came to unlock the door, and reveal the mystery of that lone, but sacred spot. His face was sunburnt, and his arms uncovered. His whole deportment gave evidence that he had been familiar and hardened to funereal woe. With a violent movement he threw open the iron door, and we stood before the entrance. Slowly we descended into the vault, and found ourselves among the dead. How

changed.! From the walls the grave sweat was
oozing forth ; the rough stone floor was covered with
human bones ; one coffin was filled with dust, and decayed limbs, another was loathsome with corruption,
while in a third, reposed the form of one who had just
been interred, the pale and lifelike corpse of a beautiful woman. The horrid effluvia, the sight of corruption, soon drove us out into the open air, and the door
was shut. Again we looked upon the beautiful monument, and read the lofty inscriptions, but there was
no beauty left. We had seen the inside of the vault,
and when we gazed upon the exterior, its chiseled
form seemed to stand in awful mockery of the sights
of woe within.

So with false religion. It is a sarcophagus. The
hand of some master-workman has been employed
upon it, and on its front are sublime inscriptions,
which men love, because they compliment our nature,
fallen and depraved as it is. But whoso entereth the
charnel will find it, not a spacious cathedral, with its
altar-fire burning, and its sweet choir chanting some
sacred song, and its worshippers bending in humble
adoration before the great God, but a house of death,
whose walls sweat drops of corruption, whose floor is
covered with its own decayed substances, and whose
tenants lie in ghastly silence, without spiritual life or
vigor.

The religion of the Bible is far different. Its

beauty is not seen until we pass the outer wall and enter the secret chambers of holiness. To the eye of the mere worldling it stands like some frowning castle, which has defied the assaults of time and change, and in impregnable strength looks down from the moun-tain upon the plains below. It appears stern, and awful in its might, and at a distance, seems to the traveler a huge pile of immovable rocks, amid which, could he climb so high, he would find but little to arrest his attention or employ his time. But let him ascend the hill, let him climb the bare and rugged side of the mountain, and as he approaches the vener-able structure, its beauty will begin to appear, and what from afar seemed great rocks piled together without order, now assumes a form of architectural beauty and grandeur. Let him enter the open gate, and explore the concealed chambers and halls, and he will find himself in the midst of unsurpassed excel-lence. As he advances, instead of confusion and de-cay, will he see order and life, and each step will re-veal to him some form of more dazzling glory than the other. The fortress is changed in his estima-tion to a gorgeous palace, fit residence for imperial monarchs.

Such being the case, it is wise, it is safe, to make the Bible our guide in all matters of sacred truth. Coming from God, it admits of no mistakes, and is a sure word of prophecy, profitable in all things.

Guided by other books men make fatal errors, and plunge headlong to destruction; guided by this, the haven of eternal rest will soon be found. Let me then exhort young men to embrace no doctrine which this book condemns. Study it for yourselves, and take not the opinions of any man, unless you find them sustained and revealed by God. The Bible was not designed for the scholar alone; it was written by God for common people; to be understood by common people; and generally the interpretations given by common people accord best with the truth as it is in Jesus. The great duties which are essential to man's salvation are revealed as clear as noon-day, and those who mistake them, are blinded by sin, or prejudiced by error. Men do not come to so many contradictory opinions because they find them in the Bible, but because they desert the Bible and wander about aided only by the dim lamp of reason. They forsake the great fountain, and drink at little turbid streams which contain poison, and produce death.

See you, yon bright sun, casting its rays upon us all! So bright that no human eye can gaze upon it. The man would be a fool who should close his windows, and shut out the light of day, and make his home dark as night, and then light one little taper, in hope to read more clearly than by the light of the " king of brightness." So he exhibits his folly, who turns from the Bible to find truth in works of human device and origin.   They are like the taper to the sun, and compared together the difference is as great.

2. The Bible will save young men from *the vices of the world*.   In regard to crime, the Bible speaks clearly and with decision, and whoever reads it, will be faithfully warned.   With this volume in his hands, no vicious man can be innocent.   The witnesses against him are found in the book which lies upon his table, and over whose pages he sometimes bends. Whatever the crime may be, it is condemned and denounced, and the severe judgments of God pronounced upon it.

Thus is it with *Sabbath-breaking*.   " Six days shalt thou labor, and do all thy work, but the seventh day is the Sabbath of the Lord thy God."   Around one seventh part of our time, around the first day, God has drawn a distinct line, separating it from all other parts of the week.   This little space of time he has reserved for himself, and enjoined the performance of religious duties, and the relinquishment of all labor.   He has declared that they who violate the Sabbath shall not prosper, and they who profane his sanctuary shall not be innocent.   On the observance of this day, the Bible is explicit, and no man can labor, or give the day to pleasure and dissipation without fearful guilt.   We are taught that Jehovah looks down from heaven with abhorrence upon a man, who not satisfied with laboring and striving for

16

gain six days, not content with giving the world six parts of the time, bestows upon, it the seventh also : steals the Sabbath from his Maker, and profanes its holy hours. If the noise and confusion of earth can ever ascend to heaven, what feelings must the angels have, as on God's day they kneel before Him in speechless adoration, while from the towns and cities below, comes up the sound of the mechanic's hammer, and the shout of the pleasure-hunting crowd.

Should we attend to the instructions of the Bible, how much more appropriately would the Sabbath be observed. Now too many employ the time in regulating their accounts, writing letters to friends, reading books which have no tendency to produce religious feelings, and others labor still more, about their farms or in their workshops. Experience and observation teach us, that this is not only wicked but altogether unprofitable. I doubt not that many a failure is the consequence of book-keeping on God's day; many a bill is unpaid because made out on the Sabbath; many a plan is defeated because formed in forbidden time. God overrules all things, and he will defeat all attempts to make money in his own time, and for one dollar which a man gains upon the Sabbath, he will lose ten, at some other time. A distinguished lawyer once observed, that he did not dare to prepare his briefs on the Sabbath, for as often as he tried it, he lost his case during the week. He became convinced that God would not allow his day to be abused and violated with impunity, and as a matter of selfish policy, deemed it wise to defer all labor until Monday. Statements like these correspond with my own experience, and I have observed that Sabbath-labor never receives the Divine blessing, and long have I expected to fail in plans of a secular nature which may have been formed on God's day. He, therefore, who observes the Bible will hallow the Sabbath, and love the sanctuary; he will delight when it arrives, to devote it to religious pursuits, and though others toil on around him, he will rest.

Thus is it with *profanity*. " Thou shalt not take the name of the Lord thy God in vain, for the Lord will not hold him guiltless who taketh his name in vain." But a moment's thought, will show that profanity is awfully prevalent. Some men who stand high in the estimation of the world, who have wealth and intelligence, seldom hesitate to blaspheme the name of Deity. The language of profanity is as common as any other expressions, and the name of God and of Christ are openly and rudely blasphemed. On the floor of our national Congress what is due to respectability and manliness, has so far been forgotten, that honorable members have been known to utter words which would disgrace a hovel of drunkenness.

From my own observation, and the testimony of others, I am led to believe that few vices are more common among young men. Persons who would not commit some other sins are betrayed into this, and practise it frequently. Indeed, so addicted are many to the practice, that they do not know when they are profane. They swear at times when they are unconscious of the fact, and often use oaths which they would deny having uttered. The Bible condemns profanity as wicked and foolish ; brands it with Divine displeasure, and positively forbids its use, and he who lives according to this book will never become addicted to it. There is something monstrous about it. To hear a man whose breath is in his nostrils, who is crushed before the moth, calling upon God to curse himself, or his wife, or his child, or his friend, is sad indeed. And yet how many do it every day ! And should God answer these requests, what would be the result ? How many would descend with oaths upon their lips to people the world of darkness and despair ?

Profanity is a useless, vulgar, wicked habit. It does no good, and much evil, and the wisdom and goodness of God can be seen in its entire prohibition. And yet with God against it, with the Bible against it, with reason and respectability again it it, it prevails extensively. It is not uncommon to see some brutal fellow, with his team loaded far too heavily, and he cursing, and beating his horse with all vengeance. How many a man has been known to curse the sidewalk against which he happens to stumble, or the unconscious door-step, against which he falls? How often do we hear men wishing their families in hell, and calling on God to send them there? doing this too, while they are in perfect good nature. Profanity is abhorrent to God, and the Bible calls upon all men to forsake it, and all good men will comply with its reasonable requirements. Cowper speaks of the vice, thus:

> "It chills my blood to hear the blest Supreme,
> Rudely appealed to on each trifling theme!
> Maintain your rank; vulgarity despise;
> To SWEAR is neither brave, polite, nor wise.
> You would not swear upon the bed of death;
> Reflect! your Maker now could stop your breath."

Thus is it with *dishonesty*. No book in stronger, clearer terms, or with more authority, condemns all falsehood, and wrong, than the Bible. "Thou shalt not steal"—"All liars shall have their part in the lake which burneth with fire," are solemn declarations of the inspired volume, and he who secures property, influence, reputation, or anything which does not belong to him, in a dishonest manner, it denounces with great severity. Other books make allowances for certain kinds of dishonesty, practised under certain circumstances, but the Bible makes no such allowances. *They* sometimes justify deception in trade; a little stretching of the truth to make a

good purchase or sale ; a little elasticity of conscience
in cases where pecuniary gain or loss is involved;
but the Bible does no such thing.   Falsehood is falsehood, whether pronounced by priest, physician, or
civilian.   Theft is theft, whether committed by genteel merchants, or highway robbers.   Crime is crime,
whether the charge be made against the possessor of
millions, or the tattered wretch who has no claim to
the earth beneath him, the heavens over him, or the
air around him.   Wrong is wrong ; kings on their
thrones, warriors at the head of marshalled armies,
statesmen in a nation's senate, fair women with jeweled fingers and flowing curls, sires and sons, mothers
and maidens, cannot make wrong, right.   There are
certain immutable principles which God cannot change
without reversing his whole nature, and these are
among them.   Hence, the Bible demands right doing
of all men, and condemns wrong in unmeasured terms,
and the young man, who has made that book the
light of his path, and the guide of his youth will do
right.   There may be a momentary profit in doing
wrong ; a present good in dishonesty, but he who re-
veres, loves, and obeys the Bible, will not do it,
though a fortune would be gained by it.   He knows
as he believes the good book, that the curse of heaven will rest upon the head of him who departs from
rectitude, and though he may prosper for awhile he
will ultimately fall.

Thus is it with *immorality*. This vice is clearly and plainly delineated, and its awful enormity exposed. No shade of the horrid crime has been left untouched by the sacred penmen, and the most blinded worshipper of the world, cannot fail to see it, in its true colors. The novice cannot deceive himself, or be deceived by others, if he will look into the perfect law of liberty, and whoso pleadeth ignorance is guilty not only for the crime, but for the very ignorance which he deems his excuse. Nor does the Bible merely forbid this vice; it goes further and holds it up to the derision of all virtuous men; it makes it look hideous and ghastly; clothes it in robes of death; and suspends over the head of the guilty one, its fearful penalties. Its requirements, are no half-way ones. They demand perfect purity of deed, word, and thought; they require stainless character. And well that it should be so. A book of morals should draw the line with unerring distinctness, so that none can cross it without feeling that he is on forbidden ground. Did Scripture leave all these matters vague and uncertain, we should be like men standing where four roads meet, not knowing which one to take, or, like a man on the ocean, without a compass, in a starless night. Thanks to God! he has not left us in darkness. A pillar of fire by night, and a cloud by day, move along the pathway of man, and if he follows that pillar of fire and cloud, he will reach the land of promise.

3. The Bible will save young men from *misery*. Man is immortal; he will live forever. A few years of his existence are to be spent on the shores of time; the remainder, the countless ages of immortality are to be spent beyond the grave. Now it is the aim of man to be happy in time and in eternity. All wish to be happy, though some pursue the road to wretchedness. The Bible tells us how we may avoid misery and secure happiness; it marks out the line of conduct in this life, that we may be happy here and hereafter. To be happy in this life, it shows us the necessity of being virtuous. Crime is attended even in this life with punishment, and no vicious man will long escape the consequences.

The drunkard is punished; he is miserable. His crime brings countless evils on his head, and involves him in shame and disgrace. He suffers intensely when the effect of intoxication has passed away, and his sober moments return. He then feels that " the way of the transgressor is hard," and sighs to escape from the chains of vice. He feels the sting, and in this life, has awful foretastes of the second death.

The gambler is miserable. His conscience will disturb him, and when away from his boon companions, he will hear the voice of some starving wife and child, whose bread he has stolen away. He must live in the midst of excitement to drown the voices which whisper in his ears such awful words. He dares not be alone, for spectre forms gather around him, and sometimes mock him, and feeling for his throbbing heart, shake it in their iron grasp.

The sensualist is miserable. "There is no peace to the wicked, saith my God," and until a man's conscience is entirely seared he will have no rest in crime. Now the Bible informs us, that to avoid the consequences of crime, we must avoid the crime itself. Misery is the result of crime, and he is unwise who expects to find one without the other.

But men are not subject to misery in this life alone. The future will be divided into different states and conditions, and some will enjoy, and others will suffer. The Bible reveals this, and teaches us how we may avoid sorrow. Suffering in another world is the consequence of sin, and some remedy for the evil must be found. The Bible presents it. It holds up the cross; shows a crucified Saviour; gives us an atoning sacrifice. The burdened sinner might search through the whole labyrinth of heathen philosophy in vain, to find an answer to the question, "How can man be just with God?" Nature, philosophy, science and art, are all mute on this awfully important theme. They shed not one ray of light upon the subject of the soul's salvation. They are dumb when man most needs instruction, and to every one who asks, "What shall I do to be saved?" they hang their heads in silence.

From them, we turn to the Bible, and find our questions answered, our doubts removed. Man can be just with God through the sufferings and death of the Incarnation ; he may be saved by trusting in the cross of Christ. Herein is the Bible most valuable. It brings life and immortality to light ; unfolds the way of hope ; dissipates the dark shadows which hang over the path of man. The Bible is valuable as a book of history, as a book of science, but more valuable as a book of LIFE, teaching how the sinner may become a saint, and his name recorded on high.

> "Let all the heathen writers join
> To form one perfect book ;
> Great God, if once compared with thine,
> How mean their writings look !
> Not the most perfect rules they give,
> Could show one sin forgiven ;
> . Nor lead a step beyond the grave ;
> But thine conducts to Heaven."

Did Socrates or Plato ever tell their disciples how the stains of guilt could be removed, and peace and pardon procured from God ? No, all was dark to them, as to the men of Africa now. They conjectured and surmised, but knew nothing. Death was a dark line which separated certainty from uncertainty, and when that line was crossed, the philosopher could go no further. Beyond death, all was darkness. But the gospel opens to us the whole matter, and settles at once all the doubts of infidelity, and the jeers of scepticism. What wonder, then, that we should love the Bible ? What wonder that we should make it the guide of our youth, and the companion of our old age ?

> " Holy Bible ! Book Divine !
> Precious treasure ! thou art mine !"

Such being the character of the Bible, such a guide in duty and in danger, it deserves our attention, and as young men, forming our opinions, and striving for usefulness, we should often consult its sacred pages. Sad mistakes are everywhere else, but there are none here.

Having considered the Bible as a perfect guide in all cases of duty and danger, I will close this discourse with a few remarks which I deem calculated to deepen any impression which may have been made upon the mind, and inspire a deeper regard for the sacred volume.

1. *All good men and many great men, have studied it, and loved it.* I know good men might have been deceived in regard to the contents of the Bible ; they may have placed a wrong estimate upon the sacred pages. Humanity is fallible, and man is liable to fall into many errors. The Koran had its believers, and has them now ; the Book of Mormon has its students and disciples ; the insane ravings of Paine are read

as truth by many around us, and gross mistakes sometimes find lodgement in pious minds. I would not
therefore urge the attachment of good men to the
Bible, as a positive argument in favor of its worth,
but must we not regard such an attachment as strong
presumptive proof that the book is worthy of our
study and belief. Should we find the good men of
this community all arrayed upon the side of a work
just issued from the press, and the bad men arrayed
against it, should we not have reason to believe the
book a good one ? Suppose on one side should be the
man of virtue, the humble Christian, the good citizen,
the worshipper of God, the friend of truth ; and on
the other side, should be marshalled the gambler, the
profane man, the libertine, the errorist, the despiser
of God, the enemy of religion, should we not at once
say, without reading the book, that it must · have
something good about it, else good men would not
love it, and bad men would not oppose it ? The very
fact that the two great classes in society, were on op-
posite sides in relation to it, would to some extent, attest its character. Now what book has been loved more
fondly by good men, and what book has been more de-
cidedly and hostilely opposed by bad men, than the
Bible. While the just, the lovely, the righteous, have
endeavored to disseminate its hallowed truth, the
wicked have endeavored to crush it. To this end, they
have passed laws, banishing it from great nations;

they have burned it publicly in the streets; they have denied its truth, and branded it as a bad production, until the friends and enemies of the book may be known, by the standard of their moral characters.

If we go back in the ages of the world we shall hear Moses, speaking thus in the name of God, of the small portion of the Bible then in the possession of men. "Lay up these my words in your heart, and in your soul, and bind them for a sign upon your hand, that they may be as frontlets between your eyes. And ye shall teach them to your children, speaking of them when thou sittest in thine house, and when thou walkest by the way; when thou liest down, and when thou risest up." God speaking to the people through Joshua says, "This book of the law, shall not depart out of thy mouth; but thou shalt meditate therein day and night, that thou mayest observe to do according to all that is written therein; for then thou shalt make thy way prosperous, and thou shalt have good success." David says, "Blessed is the man that walketh not in the counsel of the ungodly, nor standeth in the way of sinners, nor sitteth in the seat of the scornful; but his delight is in the *law of the Lord*, and in his law doth he meditate day and night." "The *law* of the Lord is *perfect*, converting the soul; the *testimony* of the Lord is *sure*, making wise the simple." "Thy *word* is a *lamp* unto my feet, and a *light* unto my path."

"The entrance of thy word giveth *light*; it giveth *understanding* unto the simple." Isaiah exclaims, "To the law, and to the testimony; if they speak not according to this word, it is because there is no light in them." Our Saviour says, "Sanctify them through thy truth; *thy word is truth.*" Paul says, "I am not ashamed of the gospel of Christ; for it is the *power of God* unto salvation, to every one that believeth; to the Jew first, and also to the Gentiles." These all speak as they are moved upon by the Holy Ghost, and their testimony is valuable, because it expresses not only the conviction of their own hearts, but also because it echoes the teachings of the Almighty.

Descending from patriarchs, prophets, and apostles, we find the "Fathers," cultivating the same respect and veneration for the Holy Scriptures. There is a long catalogue of illustrious names, gathered from "olden times," who made God's book their study and delight. High in the estimation of the church and the world, they hesitated not to declare their attachment to the blessed volume, which brings life and immortality to light. The learned Origen, the eloquent Chrysostom, the profound Augustine, with Cyprian, Tertullian, Lactantius, Arnobus, and all their pious contemporaries, have been found uttering unequivocal and manly testimony to the value of a book, from which they gathered the sublime principles on which all their writings were based.

Leaving the "Fathers," we meet with the good men of the middle centuries, and find them with the Bible in their hands, holding it with firm grasp. Even amid the flames of martyrdom, they renounced it not, but declared it to be the only sure guide for man in all matters of religious faith and practice. Jerome of Prague, while the flames curled up around him, and the fagots sent forth their burning heat, cried out, " Oh, Lord God, thou knowest how I have loved THY TRUTH." John Huss, whose ashes after he was consumed, were gathered and cast into the Rhine, died asserting the value of the Bible as a Divine revelation, and ascended to heaven amid the smoke of his own funereal pile, singing songs of praise. Cranmer, though not without his errors, loved the Bible, and died for it, and at last presented unshaken firmness, such only as the religion of the cross would inspire. Call you for witness, to the value of the Bible ? The martyrs of ten centuries would come ; from burning fagots, from bloody blocks, from damp cold prisons, from torturing inquisitions, and stand before you, a mighty throng, uttering from their bloodless lips the testimony of past ages in favor of Inspiration.

Come down to our own times, and where do we find the good and great men, to whom we are accustomed to look for words of wisdom ? They regard the Bible with veneration, and make its hallowed pages a study. They turn from the statute-book ot nations, from the various volumes of literature and science to the word of God, and find in that, more ample themes for contemplation and study. Through the long life of the venerable John Q. Adams, he made the Bible a daily study, and never allowed a day to pass without consulting its sacred teachings, and doubtless to the truths of that book, impressed upon his mind in early life, he owed much of the greatness of his after years. In all his intercourse with men, he gave evidence that his mind and heart had come into contact with the awful facts revealed in the blessed volume, and from those facts, his soul had gathered greatness and grandeur. Nor was the Sage of Quincy alone in his attachment to the Bible. Jackson, Harrison, and Polk died animated and cheered by the news of salvation, and departed this life, full of hope for another which the gospel presented before them. Nor are these alone. The records of science, art, and literature, abound with great names, who have not been ashamed of the religion of Jesus. I mention not these instances supposing that any glory is reflected upon the Bible by being believed by great men. That is impossible. As the word of God, the Bible stands far above all human attempts to honor or defame it, and man can no more confer glory upon the Bible, than can some little planet confer honor upon the bright sun around which it revolves, and from which it receives its brilliant illumination. But the fact, that great and good men have loved the Bible, is a source of encouragement to others of fewer years, and less cultivated minds.

2. The Bible has claims as *a book of history and literature.* In no other volume can we find an authentic account of the creation of the world. Historical writers do not pretend to take their readers 'back to the time, when the world rolled up out of nothingness, and became a certain and beautiful planet, revolving around the sun. They tell us nothing of the early wonders of nature, and we are in darkness (as far as they are concerned), in reference to the primal condition of our race. But the historian of the Bible has given us a beautiful, and reasonable account of the creation of land and water, bird and beast, man and woman. He has taken us along to the flood, to the burning of Sodom, to the phenomenon which attended the exodus from Egypt, to the history of the Jewish tribes, and other great events which profane writers have left untouched. Nor does this history consist of a mass of improbable statements flung together, to win the confidence of the credulous and superstitious. There is a beautiful consistency in all the Mosaic writings, which wins our confidence by appealing to reason and judgment. The worth of the Bible in this respect is inestimable, and the Old Testament should

17

have a high place in the library of every student of history.

Should some old volume be found which contained the history of the race, back to the times of Abraham and his contemporaries, and that volume embodying proof of its genuineness; with what interest would it be perused by every literary man! It would be translated into many languages, and edition after edition would issue rapidly from the press. A book we have, which goes back to the beginning; to the time when the earth, now beautified and smiling with flowers, was formless, and covered with darkness. A book we have, which furnishes us with a concise history of the world from the creation of the first Adam, to the death of the second Adam, and gives us an insight into the habits, customs, and views of men during the progress of four thousand years.

The Bible also has specimens of logic, scarcely equaled; close argument, which has never been surpassed. The Epistles abound with close reasoning, and no one who has read them attentively, can be insensible to this feature. The arguments of Paul are most convincing, and prove beyond controversy, not only the strength of his own mind, but also the strength and truth of the doctrines he taught. "The Analogy of Religion to the Constitution and Course of Nature," by Bishop Butler, has been read by many a man, simply because it is an admirable specimen of logic, a profound and sublime argument upon the subject named. And with equal propriety, may the writings of Paul be read with admiration for the force and strength of his logic, the beauty of his diction, and the grandeur of his doctrines.

The Bible also abounds with poetry of the highest order. Almost one-third of the volume is poetry of sublime character, and no uninspired man, in his most lofty flight, ever ascended so high as the monarch-muse, and the prophet-poet. There is a peculiar effect produced by singing or reading the poetry of the Bible, which the poems of uninspired men fail to produce, and they who admire the strains of Bryant, Longfellow, Hemans, and Burns, or even the greater poets, Shakspeare, Milton, Young, and Pollock, and pass by unread the inimitable poems of Isaiah, David, and Habakkuk, exhibit but little taste of head or heart. The man who claims distinction as a scholar, will not fail to be familiar with the classic poets. He will know something of Homer, Hesiod, Pindar, Anacreon, Euripides, and Sophocles; and can his education be complete without an acquaintance with the poets of the Hebrew commonwealth? Can he study Greek and Roman poets and historians, and neglect the Bible, the most sublime of all poetry, the most ancient of all history?

3. The Bible is *a* DIVINE *revelation*. In this fact consists its strength. We love it for its history and

poetry, for all the truth which it contains, but if it was not a divinely inspired book it would be comparatively worthless. But coming from God, it is clothed in robes of divinity. It gives no uncertain sound, but has the authority of the infinite Jehovah for all its teachings.

I have now presented the Bible as the young man's guide, and in bringing this series of lectures to a close, I would urge every one to adopt the inspired volume as the light of his pathway, and his constant companion. The young man is going out to battle with the vices and evils of life. The Bible is the sword which he is to carry with him. If he takes worldly wisdom, human systems of salvation, man-devised reforms, he will strike with his blunted sword upon the sides of unwounded error, in vain. But armed with the doctrines of salvation, he will be a successful warrior, and meet unharmed the assaults of all the foes of God and man. Let then our young men gird on this armor and use it well, and never put it off, or lay it down, until the battle is fought and the victory won.

THE END.

www.ingramcontent.com/pod-product-compliance
Lightning Source LLC
Chambersburg PA
CBHW031425020726
47499CB00005B/1597